Bedding the Secret Heiress

EMILIE ROSE

MILLS & BOON

First published in Great Britain 2010
Large Print edition 2010
Harlequin Mills & Boon Limited,
Eton House, 18-24 Paradise Road,
Richmond, Surrey TW9 1SR

© Emilie Rose Cunningham 2009

ISBN: 978 0 263 21580 9

Harlequin Mills & Boon policy is to use papers that
are natural, renewable and recyclable products and
made from wood grown in sustainable forests. The
logging and manufacturing process conform to the legal
environmental regulations of the country of origin.

Printed and bound in Great Britain
by CPI Antony Rowe, Chippenham, Wiltshire

EMILIE ROSE

Bestselling author and RITA® Award finalist Emilie Rose lives in her native North Carolina with her four sons and two adopted mutts. Writing is her third (and hopefully her last) career. She's managed a medical office and run a home day care, neither of which offers half as much satisfaction as plotting happy endings. Her hobbies include gardening and cooking (especially cheesecake). She's a rabid country music fan because she can find an entire book in almost any song. She is currently working her way through her own "Bucket List" which includes learning to ride a Harley. Visit her website at www.emilierose.com

Letters can be mailed to P.O. Box 20145, Raleigh, NC 27619., and readers can email her at EmilieRoseC@aol.com

This one's for LaShawn

Thank you for teaching me to dance
like nobody's watching.

One

Here we go again.

Lauren expelled an exasperated breath and punched the elevator button for the top floor. Getting called to her half brother's office was a lot like the way she imagined getting called to the principal's office might have been if she'd ever dared to get into trouble in school.

Trent didn't want her here—an opinion he'd made abundantly clear in the six weeks since their mother had used her position as president of the board of directors and the company's largest stockholder to force him to hire Lauren as a pilot for Hightower Aviation Management Corporation.

Trent couldn't fire her, but he'd done everything in his power to make her quit. He seemed to relish personally doling out lousy assignments no one else wanted: the obnoxious clients, redeye flights and landings at substandard airports. Today's summons was bound to deliver more of the same. But he'd soon learn she could handle anything he dished out.

The elevator stopped on the third floor and two suit-clad women boarded. Security badges labeled them HAMC employees. Their cool gazes raked Lauren's clothing, making her wish she'd taken time to don her pilot's uniform, but she could hardly ride her Harley in a skirt. And if these two had received a memo from her half brother ordering them to make her work life a living hell, they'd discover she didn't care.

She'd never had anyone hate her before, but besides the chill factor from other employees, she had three of her four newly discovered half siblings wishing she'd disappear. Who could blame them? She was a walking, talking reminder of their mother's infidelity, the child Jacqueline Hightower had borne to her pilot lover while still married to their father, an embarrassing dirty secret Jacqui had managed to keep tucked away in another state for twenty-five years.

The door opened on the tenth floor and the sour-faced women disembarked. As the doors closed again Lauren fought the urge to hit the down button, go back to Florida and forget her new family. Too bad the Hightowers, bless their cold, moneygrubbing hearts, were the only relatives she had left. For her father's sake, for Falcon Air's sake, she'd suck it up and deal with any and all unpleasant attitudes until she had the information about her father's death that only her mother could provide.

Had he committed suicide or had his crash been an accident? Her mother had been the last to talk to him. If he'd been considering something so desperate, surely he'd have given Jacqui some clues? But, damn her, Jacqui wasn't talking. And until the Federal Aviation Administration, the National Transportation Safety Board and the insurance company finished their investigations Lauren's hands were bound by red tape.

She didn't want to believe her father had deliberately ended his life, but the alternative was even more horrific. She'd helped him build the experimental plane he'd crashed. If his accident had been caused by an equipment failure, then she could be partly to blame.

Grief and guilt squeezed her lungs and burned her throat. She swallowed the caustic emotions. The elevator doors opened to the executive floor. She took a deep, bracing breath and readied herself for yet another battle.

Only for you, Daddy.

Tucking her riding gloves into the motorcycle helmet dangling from her fingertips, she stepped out of the compartment. Her lug-soled Harley boots sank into thick carpeting, another reminder that she wasn't in Daytona anymore. The luxurious Hightower high-rise was a far cry from the concrete floors and drafty metal hangars she'd grown up in.

She stretched her lips into as big a smile as she could muster and unzipped her jacket as she approached "The Sphinx's" desk. Getting her brother's administrative assistant to crack an expression—*any* expression—had become a mission. No success this time, either. The woman should play poker for a living.

"Hi, Becky. The boss wants to see me." Becky—a warm and friendly name for a cold woman. Talk about irony.

Becky looked pointedly at her watch. "I'll inform him you've *finally* arrived."

Lauren bit her tongue. Trent was lucky she'd answered her cell phone once she'd recognized his office number on caller ID. But she *was* making an effort to be civil.

She studied the fresh-cut flower arrangement on the credenza while Becky did her thing. The massive bouquet had probably cost as much as an hour's worth of jet fuel. Pretty, but a total waste of money, in Lauren's opinion.

"You may go in." Becky's stiff words pulled Lauren's attention away from the cloying blooms that reminded her of her father's funeral.

Such formality. Back home Lauren had knocked and entered her father's and Uncle Lou's offices at Falcon Air without playing the stupid Simon Says game. They'd had no secrets…or so she'd thought.

"Thanks." Lauren pushed open the heavy six-panel door of what she'd come to call the throne room. Her half brother sat behind his football field–size desk in his massive leather chair looking as arrogant and unwelcoming as ever. "You called?"

Darn straight he had. He'd interrupted her motorcycle ride along Knoxville's back roads. He couldn't know how much she'd been enjoying blowing away her tension by cruising along the curvy, hilly terrain after a lifetime of Daytona's flat, straight streets. She'd be damned if she'd let him know he'd ruined her day.

His upper lip hitched in disapproval as he took in her riding gear.

The back of Lauren's neck pricked. She turned quickly to her right. A raven-haired thirtysomething man rose from the visitor chair. Alert dark eyes lasered into hers before his gaze taxied over her black leather jacket, pants, boots and back to the helmet hanging from her left hand. He had a power and charisma thing going that she would have found attractive in other circumstances.

While he assessed her, she cataloged his above-average height, his wide shoulders and a don't-mess-with-me stubborn jaw. From the perfect fit of his black suit she guessed he was an HAMC customer. And if he was here for her, then he was probably also an arrogant jackass no matter how handsome he might be. Big brother had yet to assign her any other kind of client.

Taking the initiative, she offered her hand. "I'm Lauren Lynch. And you are…?"

"Gage Faulkner." His hand engulfed hers in a firm, warm grip that made it difficult to inhale. She wondered how he'd managed to squish the air from her lungs with a handshake and how to abort that little trick. She blinked and gently tugged her arm, but he didn't release her.

There was no welcome in his expression as he looked beyond her shoulder to her half brother. "She looks too young to be a commercial pilot."

"You know I'd never set you up with someone who wasn't qualified," Trent replied.

Irked at being talked about as if she wasn't there, Lauren gave her wrist a quick twist and hard yank, breaking Faulkner's hold the way she'd been taught by an airport security guard she'd once dated. "I'm twenty-five. I've been licensed since my sixteenth birthday, and I've logged more than ten thousand hours."

Faulkner's cool gaze found hers again, and she noted flecks of gold in the brown of his irises. A tight smile twitched his lips. Nice lips. Kissable lips.

Client.

The warning flashed in her brain like airfield lamps, shutting down that runway. Getting involved with a client was grounds for firing. Was Trent setting her up with a gorgeous guy to take her down? She wouldn't put it past him since all his other strategies had failed.

She cut her brother a suspicious look. Did he think she couldn't resist an attractive face? Knucklehead didn't know she'd been fending off men since puberty. Not that she was beautiful or anything, but she wasn't ugly, and the man-to-woman ratio at small airports left a lot of men lonely and looking. She'd had her father and Uncle Leo as growling watchdogs, but they hadn't always been around. She'd learned a few lessons the hard way.

Trent hit her with his usual joy-killing glare. "Gage, please excuse Lauren's attire. I assure you HAMC has a dress code."

Her spine snapped erect. "It's my day off. I wasn't sitting at home in my uniform waiting for your call. When you said urgent I came straight in instead of making you cool your jets while I went home to change."

Faulkner choked a noise that sounded a lot like a laugh. She shot him a warning look. He wiped his jaw, hiding his mouth, but his eyes glimmered with amusement. For some reason that irritated Lauren even more. Their family feud was none of his business.

"Sit down, Lauren." Trent's superior tone set her teeth on edge. One of these days someone was going to knock the landing gear out from under his ego. She hoped she'd be around to witness him biting the asphalt. Unlikely she'd have the pleasure since she planned to vacate Knoxville and abandon her polar bear relatives as soon as she got what she needed from her mother.

Lauren sat in the guest chair beside Faulkner's. A subtle but pleasant trace of his spicy cologne teased her nose. She focused on her brother, the arrogant butt-head in charge. "What's so urgent it couldn't wait until I clock in tomorrow?"

"Gage needs a pilot. You're it."

That was her job, the job of any HAMC pilot, for that matter. So why did that telling itch crawling up her neck warn her that this wasn't a regular assignment?

"What and where will I be flying?"

Probably an albatross to some mosquito-infested, potholed, mud runway or an unheated cargo carrier to the frozen tundra, if her half brother continued true to form.

"Gage will use a variety of aircraft, depending on the length of his trip and the size of the team accompanying him. The majority of the time you'll fly a small to midsize jet, but occasionally a helicopter or Cessna."

Excitement gurgled through her before she could dam it. The job description sounded too good to be true—especially since Hightower Aviation limited its pilots to flying only one type of aircraft so they'd be familiar with the controls. That had been her primary grievance since she'd arrived. She lived for variety and loved testing the abilities of different airplanes.

Her half brother was being nice *and* bending company policy. Had his conscience finally kicked in? She studied his impassive face, not buying altruism as his motive for one second.

"Trent assures me you can handle whatever I need."

Faulkner's velvety voice snagged her attention, winching her gaze back to him. He meant flightwise, didn't he?

Her stomach did a weird flutter thing that made her question the sanitation grade of the roadside diner she and her neighbors had stopped at for lunch.

"I'm certified to fly almost anything civilian with wings or rotors. Mastering different aircraft is kind of a hobby of mine." *More like an obsession.* "What's the catch?"

Did she imagine a quick stiffening of those broad shoulders? The slight hesitation as he pursed that attention-getting mouth? "If you fly for me, you'll be on call 24/7, beginning tomorrow morning at five."

Again, standard procedure for HAMC pilots. They all flew on four hours notice or less. Something wasn't right here. "And?"

"You'll be working exclusively for Gage."

Trent's statement had her head whipping his way as the meaning of his bombshell sank in. "You're taking me off rotation?"

"I'm giving you a special assignment."

The bully was farming her out to someone else, and there wasn't one thing she could say about it in front of the client, unless she wanted to get fired for insubordination. She refused to mouth off and give Trent the satisfaction of an easy way out.

Gritting her teeth, she fought her seething anger. Being cut from the schedule was like being sent to her room or put in time out. And damn it, she hadn't done anything wrong to earn such shoddy treatment. Working for only one client would limit her hours and her pay. Her mother would never allow—

No. She wouldn't go to her mother. Their relationship was too new, too tentative and too volatile for Lauren to ask Jacqui to choose sides between her oldest son and her youngest daughter, and Lauren couldn't afford to alienate her mother yet. This turf war was between her and Trent, and Lauren refused to let him win.

Tightening her grip on her helmet strap rather than around her half brother's thick neck as she'd prefer, she stared him down. "I'll be the pilot-in-command instead of first officer?"

Her idiot brother had limited her to flying as first officer instead of the pilot-in-command. She hadn't flown in the copilot seat in years, and the pilots he'd made her fly with often had fewer qualifications than she did. But she'd accepted the entry-level position while she earned her certifications in the models and equipment new to her. She could endure any indignity as long as it benefited her in the end—even playing nice with her mother.

Trent tossed his pen onto his blotter. "None of the aircraft Gage has requested require a copilot."

He threw her a sweet bone of concession to offset the bitter deal he was forcing down her throat. "None of your other HAMC pilots is assigned a one-on-one job."

"My other pilots don't have your…varied experience." He made the comment sound like an insult instead of the compliment it would have been coming from any other employer.

Don't let him rattle you. You know that's what he wants. "How long is the assignment?"

"For as long as Gage needs you. Becky has your immediate schedule and plane assignments." Trent rose and indicated the door, dismissing her.

She'd learned early on that arguing with Trent was a waste of time. Eager to escape the blockhead's presence as well as see what and where she'd be flying, Lauren sprang to her feet. The upside was HAMC had some sweet planes that her brother had yet to let her touch. Maybe she'd get behind the controls of a few.

Faulkner unfolded his long body beside her, making her aware of his height and the smooth, athletic way he moved. He towered over her as he offered his hand. "I look forward to flying with you, Lauren."

His chilly tone belied his words and made her wonder if Trent had poisoned yet another mind against her. She reluctantly put her hand in his. That same breath-stealing surge shot through her again, and something flickered in his eyes, making her wonder if he felt it, too—whatever *it* was. Didn't matter. That wasn't a trip she'd be taking.

"I'll do my best to deliver smooth, punctual flights." Ripping her hand free, she spun on her heel and hustled her boots out of the throne room. Killjoy Trent shadowed her to The Sphinx's desk.

"Lauren, Gage is a close personal friend." He pitched his voice low enough not to carry back through the open door of his office. "Don't blow this or you're out of a job."

Ah. The catch. She rocked back on her heels. Trent had assigned her to work for a spy—one who would help him find grounds to get rid of her.

Wasn't that a show of brotherly love? She bit back the urge to tell him to kiss her butt. But she'd deal with Trent's tricks until she got what she needed. Then she'd tell him what he could do with his big head and bad attitude.

"Piece of cake, big brother. I'll treat your buddy like precious cargo."

The obvious grinding of his teeth when she called him *brother* nearly made her laugh out loud. Score one for baby sister. But she knew better than to let down her guard. This battle was far from over.

* * *

Angel or badass?

Gage's gaze tracked Lauren Lynch out of the room. The woman was a walking contradiction with her big teal eyes, flawless honey complexion and the black leather biker gear hugging her lean curves.

The bone-jarring effect of her touch had been an unwelcome surprise. Even if she weren't Trent's sister, she was too young for him, and he had no time or inclination for complications—not when he was this close to reaching his goal of having Faulkner Consulting be the best in the industry and having six million in secure investments.

"Your announcement was a bit premature," Gage said the moment Trent closed the office door. "You haven't convinced me to fly with Hightower Aviation yet."

"I will."

Maybe. Maybe not. But he'd give Trent a chance to state his case. He owed him that much. "Lauren gives you a hard time."

"But she's smart enough to keep from crossing the line and giving me grounds to fire her. She has my mother wrapped around her little finger."

"Are you sure? Jacqueline's pretty sharp. You have to give her credit for keeping Hightower Aviation from going under after her father died and yours dropped the ball. She even managed to take HAMC international by convincing her jet-setting friends to employ your services on their pleasure jaunts."

Trent sat behind his desk. "Mom's been hood-winked this time."

"How does this involve me? Your message said you needed my help, but you left out the details."

"Eighteen months ago Mom flew to Daytona. Shortly thereafter she began making large cash withdrawals of between twenty and thirty thousand on a regular basis. She's returned to Daytona bimonthly since then."

"Is it company money?" Embezzlement would be bad news.

"No, it's my mother's personal funds, but her accountant called me with a heads-up. I ordered him to alert me to any unusual transactions. Remember my father's stunt? And yours?"

Gage's gut tightened. "I remember."

He might have only been ten when his father overextended himself, borrowing against his business and their home until he'd lost everything, but living in the family car for six months wasn't something Gage would ever forget. Trent was the only one Gage had ever trusted with those details.

"Why would Jacqueline suddenly go off the deep end now?"

"That's what I'm trying to figure out. If Mom's judgment is faulty or if she's getting senile, then I need to get her off the board of directors before she does serious damage."

"You're going to need more than speculation to unseat her."

Trent glanced at the papers on his desk. "Mom's spending and visits to Daytona escalated a few months before Lauren moved to Knoxville. Lauren is from Daytona. My guess is she discovered her birth mother had deep pockets and decided to cozy up and dip her hands into them."

"Lauren doesn't look like a con artist."

"Don't let those big blue eyes and her innocent girl-next-door look fool you. If I didn't have good reason to suspect she's tapped my mother's financial vein, I wouldn't have called you."

Trent, like Gage, wasn't the type to ask for help. That his friend had called meant he was desperate. "If your mother is channeling money to your baby sister—"

"*Half* sister," Trent corrected. "And the only reason I believe that is because I had a DNA test done during her employment screening process."

"Is that legal and does Lauren know?"

"I doubt she knows, but she signed a waiver allowing us to test for whatever we wanted when she took the job. I tested for everything."

"She came up clean?"

"Unfortunately. Ditching her would have been much easier if her drug tests or background check had revealed even a hint of something questionable. Hell, even her credit history is clear."

Trent really had it in for the girl, but he'd never been the type to overreact or jump to conclusions. Because of his family's wealth Trent had always been a target for gold diggers, and his radar for them was unmatched. He must have good cause for his suspicions about Lauren.

"You've asked your mother about the cash?"

Trent nodded. "And she locked up tighter than Fort Knox. If she has nothing to hide, then why keep secrets?"

"I hear you." But Gage lived by the opposite theory. He didn't believe in revealing anything unless required. "What about Lauren? Did you ask her why she relocated?"

"Lauren gave me some bullshit about her father wanting her to meet her Hightower siblings as a reason for her move to Knoxville, and she claims she knows nothing about the money."

"Why wouldn't your mother have given Lauren money sooner? Why wait twenty-five years?"

"Maybe Mom didn't know where Lauren was

or she could have been giving her smaller amounts over the years that didn't catch the accountant's notice. But we never heard a whisper about Mom's little mistake until she showed up on our doorstep, pilot credentials in hand and expecting to waltz into a job. Do you know how selective Hightower Aviation is in hiring?"

"Lauren doesn't meet your standards?"

Trent's scowl deepened. "Other than her lack of a college degree, she exceeds them. But, Gage, she's too damned young to have the résumé she's claiming. I just haven't been able to prove she's lying. Hell, I've checked and rechecked her credentials and put her through a battery of physical and mental testing, looking for any reason to reject her. I even forced her to sit through hours of training in a flight simulator before allowing her in a real cockpit. But the little smart-ass aced all the tests and refused to quit."

That earned her a dose of grudging respect. "Maybe she's simply a good pilot."

"Nobody's that good at that age."

"You were."

Trent's entire body tensed and Gage regretted his words. Trent had practically been raised in a cockpit. He'd been eager to join the Air Force as a pilot after college, but his father had nearly destroyed HAMC by incurring gambling debts that had jeopardized the company. Trent had been forced to abandon his military career plans to clean up his father's mess. By the time he'd dug HAMC out of the negative spiral Trent's dream had been supplanted by the necessity of remaining CEO of HAMC.

"I apologize. I shouldn't have brought that up."

"Forget it. It was a long time ago. I'm over it." Trent cleared his throat. "Here's what I know. My mother hid her pregnancy then gave Lauren up for adoption to her natural father rather than tell my father she'd gotten knocked up by one of her lovers."

"Your father must have known. As Jacqueline's husband he would have been Lauren's legal father despite her biological paternity. He would have had to agree to relinquish."

Trent raked a hand through hair a shade lighter

than his half sister's dirty blond. "Dad claims he doesn't remember the 'incident' or signing any forms. My guess is he would have done anything to keep my mother funding his gambling addiction. Remember, HAMC was a smaller operation back then, and the majority of Hightower money came from my mother's family. Consequently, Dad turned a blind eye to all her affairs. My grandfather probably greased the wheels to keep things quiet."

"All valid points." But despite her biker gear and attitude, Lauren didn't give off the greedy bitch vibe. "Lauren doesn't look like a woman being showered with gifts from a wealthy benefactress. She's not wearing jewelry, makeup or designer clothes."

"She drives a twenty-thousand-dollar motorcycle, a sixty-thousand-dollar truck and flies a quarter-million-dollar airplane. What does that tell you?"

That she'd fooled him. But hadn't he learned the hard way that women often promised one thing and schemed to get something else altogether? Gage's anger stirred. "She's damned good at hiding her avaricious nature. But I repeat, what does this have to do with me?"

"Until I can get the cash flow dammed I need you to keep Lauren out of my hair and away from my mother."

"And from your phone message I gather you believe I can do that by using Hightower Aviation's services for free."

Trent nodded. "Flying a private jet rather than a commercial airline will save you time. You've canceled our last three dinners because you claimed you needed to be in two places at once due to two of your team members being out on parental leave."

"Right." Yet another reason why Gage would never have children. They were a distraction. Recent family additions had turned two of his best consultants—one male, one female—into babbling, sleep-deprived fools. He wasn't letting anyone get between him and a steady, secure income. And he didn't want anyone depending on him.

"I can help you, and in turn, you can help me," Trent added. "If I don't cut off the money leak, then Mom could be tempted to dip into Hightower Aviation funds the way my father did. For the next two or three months you'll be out of town more than in. If Lauren is your pilot, she will be, too. That works for me."

Gage's collar suddenly felt like a noose. As convenient as having a plane at his beck and call might be, he'd never been comfortable with the freeloader role—a circumstance Trent knew only too well. "Faulkner Consultants can afford HAMC's services. Draw up a contract."

"No way. We both know how you feel about large capital expenses. I explained on the message machine before you came in. This one's on me."

"You laid out a sketchy plan, but there's more involved here than you let on."

"Damn it, Gage, get the chip off your shoulder. How many times do I have to tell you that you don't owe me or my family anything? Trust me on this. If you can occupy Lauren for a couple of months, *I'll* owe *you.* Keeping the parasite away from my mother is going to save me more money in the long run than you leasing a plane or buying fractional ownership in one is going to generate."

Gage's molars ground together. He'd swallowed more humble pie than he could handle in a lifetime. Never again. "Trent—"

"I need your help, man. Don't make me beg."

Gage ran a hand over the tense muscles of his neck. "Then we do it my way. Draw up a short-term contract. If it saves me time and money, then I'll renew when the term ends. If not, I'll at least know I paid my way."

Trent's jaw jacked up. "That's not necessary."

"It is for me."

Trent's mouth opened, but closed again without further argument. "Fine. If you can manage to find out Lauren's intentions while you're at it, that would be even better."

Gage recoiled. He'd been waiting thirteen years for an opportunity to repay the debt he owed his former college roommate, but there were some boundaries he wouldn't cross even for his best friend. "I won't be your snitch."

"I'm not asking you to sleep with her or marry her to get information. Just find out how long she intends to be a boil on my ass."

"If Lauren is the mercenary bitch you claim, then I'll tell you what you need to know to protect yourself and your assets. But that's it. Nothing more."

Trent's brow creased as he considered Gage's offer. "Deal."

Two

The rasp of a suit-clad leg brushing her shoulder shattered Lauren's concentration. She looked up from entering data into the navigation screen as Gage squeezed through the narrow opening between the cockpit and passenger cabin.

"Mr. Faulkner, we're about to take off. Please go back to your seat and buckle in."

"Call me Gage, and I prefer sitting up front." He folded into the copilot chair on her right.

"I'd rather you stay in the passenger cabin."

He reached for the seat belt and clicked it in

place. "Are you afraid I'll see you skip a step in preflight preparations, Lauren?"

Her teeth clicked together. He'd been an aggravation from the moment he'd insisted on carrying his own bags on board. The HAMC rulebook stated that her job as pilot was to greet each passenger and personally carry on and properly stow any weighted objects they brought along. The last thing she needed to do was give her half brother a stupid infraction to use against her.

"I never skip steps."

"Good. Do you have a spare headset?"

The mercury in her mental thermometer climbed and her ears burned. "We're flying a Cessna Mustang because you wanted to work on the way to Baton Rouge in the luxury of a spacious cabin. You even requested no flight attendant on board so you wouldn't have interruptions."

He kept his gaze leveled on hers, not giving an inch. An odd tension seeped into her midsection.

"I awoke hours before my alarm went off this

morning and accomplished what I needed to do before I left for the airport. I'd rather sit up front where I can see."

Disliking the invasion of her space and the breach in protocol, she grappled for patience and stretched her lips into a smile. "There are six windows in the back. Besides, on an overcast day there's not a lot to see from thirty thousand feet. I'll be flying above the cloud deck."

"I'll take my chances."

She counted to three, trying to rein in her temper. "The seats in the cabin are larger, more comfortable and they recline. You could catch up on your missed sleep during the flight."

"Not necessary."

Her knuckleheaded half brother had probably asked his spy to annoy her as much as possible, and judging by the gleam in Faulkner's dark eyes and the stubborn set of his jaw he knew he was getting under her skin like a splinter.

"If you'd mentioned your preference for sitting up front earlier, we could have cleared it with the office and conserved fuel by taking a smaller plane rather than fly five empty seats."

"That would have cost us speed and time."

She couldn't argue with facts. A smaller plane would have flown slower and lower than HAMC's smallest jet. "Allowing passengers in the cockpit is against HAMC protocol."

"Call your brother."

"Half brother. I can't. As you no doubt know, he's tied up in a board meeting all morning, and his dragon lady won't put calls through."

"Then I guess you're stuck with me in the copilot seat."

But she would take this up with Trent when she returned home. Her father's number one rule echoed in her head. *The customer is always right—unless safety is involved.* Resigned to Faulkner's unwanted company, she conceded, "There's a spare headset beneath your seat."

Most pilots, including her, brought their own equipment, but Hightower Aviation always provided extras. She hated to admit it, but HAMC went first-class all the way by providing luxuries for its passengers and crew that Falcon Air couldn't afford.

Gage removed the gear from the bag and plugged the headset into the appropriate jack as if he'd done this before, then sat back in his seat with his long-fingered hands relaxed on his thighs.

Muscular thighs, not desk jockey thighs.

Client.

She diverted her stray thoughts, assumed her strictest flight instructor persona and met his gaze. "If you have sunglasses, put them on. Don't speak until I tell you I've finished with the control tower, and don't touch anything that doesn't belong to you. You may not need to concentrate during the flight, but I do if you want me to keep this baby in the air."

The corners of his lips twitched, and she almost smiled back. "That would be preferable to the alternative."

Of crashing. Like her father.

The swift stab of pain caught her off guard. She squelched her grief and focused on entering her flight plan data into the computer. It took twenty minutes to finish her preflight check, get clearance and put the plane in the air—twenty minutes during which Gage silently observed her every move like an eagle waiting to strike.

When she was in the cockpit she was all business all the time. Her father had taught her that was the only way young pilots lived to become old pilots. An airplane was the one place she knew she was good—*damned* good. But Gage made her second-guess her actions instead of doing them instinctively. Before him, no other passenger or pilot had ever disrupted her concentration.

She hated being conscious of each shift of his body in the leather seat, the rise and fall of his chest and the spicy tang of his cologne. And while she couldn't hear him moving and breathing through her noise-canceling headphones, she could feel his presence in the close quarters of the cockpit.

His steady regard made her very aware of her scraped-back hair, lack of makeup and unpainted, short-clipped nails. He made her feel feminine. And lacking. Not a pleasant combination.

Once she reached cruising altitude, she glanced at him and straight into those dark eyes. Her stomach swooped as if she'd hit an air pocket and the plane had dropped. "You can talk now. If you must. Speak in a regular tone of voice. I'll hear you loud and clear through the headphones."

"Why flying?" he fired back without hesitation.

A familiar question. She shrugged. "I grew up around airports and never wanted to do anything else."

"What did you do before joining Hightower Aviation?"

Her half brother had probably asked Gage to grill her. Careerwise, she had nothing to hide, nothing that she hadn't put in her résumé. Still, unsure of his agenda, she chose her words carefully. "Fifty percent of the time I'm a flight instructor. The rest of the time I fly charter jets for Falcon Air."

"What's Falcon Air?"

He certainly had a talent for faking genuine interest while pumping her for information. "My father's charter plane company."

"Is he running it while you're gone?"

She flinched as the unintentional arrow sank deep into her chest. Would the pain ever stop? "No. He recently…died. My uncle is acting as general manager."

"My condolences." Cool words devoid of emotion.

"What is it you do exactly, Mr.—Gage?" Not that she cared, but she'd rather talk about him than herself and risk inadvertently revealing something she shouldn't. If word got out that her father might have committed suicide, then Falcon Air would lose business. Their clients would not be inclined to hire a company that flew faulty planes—or worse, engage a pilot who might take a deliberate header into the Everglades with them on board. And finances were iffy enough already.

"I'm a business consultant. I assess companies and make recommendations for improvements, specifically targeting ways to make them financially secure by eliminating waste and increasing productivity."

"You do that internationally?"

"Yes. Did you decide to search for your birth mother after your father's death?"

She stifled her frustration as he volleyed the topic back to her. "No. She came to me."

"You must have been surprised to meet her."

"Meet her? I don't know what Trent told you, but I've known Jacqui all my life. I wasn't aware my father's on-again-off-again girlfriend was my mother until my eighteenth birthday when she and my father decided to share the information. I didn't know Jacqui was married until after my father's funeral when she told me my father wanted me to meet my sib—her other children."

His eyes narrowed. "You've known Jacqueline for years?"

"Yes."

"What kind of mother was she? A generous one, I'll bet."

More innuendo. She rolled her eyes and then scanned the sky for traffic. She'd had a load of the same attitude from all but one of her half siblings. They seemed to think she was looking for handouts and a free ride, but what she wanted was something Jacqui could give her without putting a dent in the Hightower heirs' inheritance.

"I just told you Jacqui wasn't a mother at all. And no, she didn't shower me with expensive gifts. My father wouldn't have allowed it. Nor would I have accepted them."

The disbelief written all over his face ticked her off. One, because this stranger had judged and assumed the worst of her, and two, because Trent had probably filled Gage's ears with lies. It was one thing for her half brother to resent her and hate her guts, but it was low and crass of him to spread his poison professionally. She knew he had. Otherwise, the other HAMC employees wouldn't give her the cold shoulder.

"Jacqueline wanted you to join Hightower Aviation?"

"This is a temporary gig. Jacqui knows I'm going back to Falcon in a few months."

"Why a few months?"

"Why twenty questions?" she countered.

"I'm curious. Most people wouldn't willingly

walk away from the level of luxury associated with the Hightower name."

"I'm not most people, Mr. Faulkner, and I'm not a Hightower. If we're going to work together, you'd better get used to that. And if Trent put you up to this interrogation, then please tell him he'll have to come to me himself for answers."

Not that she'd ever reveal the full truth behind her presence in Knoxville. Her reasons for being here were no one's business but hers, and she'd be damned if she'd feed Gage Faulkner anything he could carry back to Trent to be used against her. If she did, it could destroy Falcon Air, and then she'd have nothing to return home to.

Gage's gut told him Lauren was hiding something, and his gut was never wrong.

She'd clammed up as soon as the conversation about her mother had become interesting, and no amount of questioning, subtle or otherwise, had gotten her to open up again during the flight. But getting answers was his specialty.

He flashed the ID badge Hightower Aviation

had provided for him at the security guard. The man waved him through the doors to the tarmac. "Have a good trip, sir."

Gage nodded his thanks, exited the terminal of the small suburban airport and approached the jet. Trent had been right. Traveling via private carrier was a lot less hassle than flying a commercial airline. Faster in, faster out allowed for more time on the job and less in transit. Gage had to admit he liked the efficiency.

Tired, but satisfied with the preliminary information he'd gathered on the project he'd come to Baton Rouge to assess, he checked his watch. Because of the security check-in time savings he was an hour early. When he'd left Lauren seven hours ago she hadn't seemed concerned at being stranded with nothing to do for the majority of the day. In fact, her eyes had sparkled and her body had practically vibrated with excitement as if she couldn't wait to be rid of him. Not a common occurrence for him. Women—when he made time for them—enjoyed his company.

But not Lauren.

She'd given him her cell number and asked him to call when he finished his business and headed toward the airport, claiming it would allow her to prepare the plane for takeoff before he arrived. He hadn't called. Arriving early fit in with his plan to catch her doing whatever it was she did to fill her day. Her activities might give some clue as to her intentions.

The door to the Cessna stood open and the stairs were down as if waiting for visitors on this warm October day. He climbed on board, and the plane rocked slightly under his weight. Lauren abruptly sat upright in one of the plush leather passenger seats and lowered the feet she'd had tucked under her to the floor. She had a laptop computer resting on her thighs. "You're back."

"Did I interrupt something?"

"No. I was just…killing time."

But not in a relaxed way, judging by the tension around her mouth and eyes.

The setting sun streamed through the window behind her, painting coppery streaks in the slightly disheveled dark blond curtain hanging past her shoulders. Her uniform hat rested on a nearby table and her jacket draped a seat back. She hastily closed the open top button of her shirt, covering a V of pale honeyed skin.

"You were supposed to call so I could get the preflight done and get you into the air faster."

She seemed flustered. Was she hiding something?

"My mind was on work." Not a lie, just not the entire truth and a necessary omission if he were going to play sleuth. He stowed his briefcase in the compartment she'd shown him earlier.

Her eyes narrowed as if she didn't believe him, and then she typed a few keys. A few seconds later her eyebrows and the corners of her lips dipped. "Jacqui says hello."

Alarms sounded in his brain. "You were online with your mother?"

"Yes." A flicker of irritation crossed her face. "Instant messaging."

Lauren closed her computer, tucked it into a leather bag by her feet and rose. She twisted her hair up, clipping it into place then she snatched up her hat and set it on her head. "She remembers you from your college visits with Trent."

Jacqueline would. The Hightower family had often included Gage on vacations—probably because Trent had told them that Gage had nowhere else to go when the dorms shut down for the holidays. He couldn't exactly join his father because his parent was usually living in a homeless shelter or on the street. Gage had no idea where his mother had gone. The old humiliation still burned his pride.

"I wouldn't have pegged Jacqueline as the instant messaging type."

"You'd be wrong. She's quite techno-savvy."

That translated into trouble. He could physically keep the women apart, but he couldn't prevent them from connecting via cyberspace when all of HAMC's planes had wireless access. That was something neither he nor Trent had anticipated. The situation would require reevaluation and a new strategy.

Lauren stowed her computer case in the compartment behind the pilot's seat and locked it down. "I refueled after we landed, but I'll need about thirty minutes to get ready for takeoff."

"No rush. In fact, why don't we have dinner first?"

Lauren's crisp, economical movements stopped abruptly with her uniform jacket half-on. Her eyes turned wary. "Dinner?"

He needed to find out exactly how tight she and her mother had become. "I passed a Brazilian steak place on the way to the airport that looked interesting."

She licked her lips as if tempted, and his gaze involuntarily followed the sweep of her pink tongue. The muscles in his gut tightened. He dammed the reaction. Lauren might look as fresh-faced as the proverbial girl next door, but the intelligence in her eyes and her quiet confidence as she operated the multimillion dollar aircraft belied her being uncomplicated.

She finished putting on her coat and buttoned it up to her neck. "I'm more than happy to delay takeoff until after you've eaten. It'll give me time to prepare for—"

"Join me, Lauren."

She shook her head. "Fraternizing with clients is against HAMC rules."

"I'll call Trent and clear it."

She blinked. Why had he never noticed her long lashes before? "Thank you, but I've already eaten."

He didn't believe her. "What did you have?"

She hesitated. "A sandwich from the airstrip cantina."

"Then I'll have the same. Keep me company." At least that would keep her from hooking up with her mother again while he was out of sight.

A stubborn expression shut down her face. "No thank you, Mr. Faulkner. I'll prepare the plane while you eat."

He had the distinct impression she didn't want to be alone with him. He had every intention of finding out why and what she had to hide.

The crunch of a shoe behind her in the misty, dark parking lot kicked Lauren's adrenaline into high gear. She spun around, ready to gouge an assailant with her keys if necessary.

Trent stepped into the murky light of a lamppost and stopped two yards away when he saw her aggressive stance.

Lauren's hammering pulse slowed, but her irritation rose. After a full day's flying and dealing with Gage's scrutiny, she was too tired for a back-biting confrontation. She needed to get home and call her mother and then her uncle. For five full seconds she debated ignoring her half brother, climbing into her truck and driving off. But she'd never been one to back down from a bully.

She lowered her keys. "You need better lighting in your parking area. If I were trigger-happy and had pepper spray, you'd be on your knees howling by now."

Trent's gaze went from her to her truck and back. "I'll mention your concerns to security."

Sure he would. Impatient, she tapped her toe. "Did you need something?"

"Lauren, if Gage wants to sit in the cockpit he can. If he asks you to eat dinner with him, do it. Do whatever he says."

His my-word-is-law tone raised her hackles

and sent a trickle of unease through her. "Exactly how far do you expect me to go to keep the customer happy?"

His head jerked back and his nostrils flared. "I'm not asking you to do anything illegal or immoral."

"You're asking me to violate HAMC rules. I want you to spell out your expectations—in writing. Preferably signed and notarized."

"What? You don't trust me, little sister?"

"Half sister." She shouldered her flight bag. "You've made it clear from day one that I'm unwelcome here. I'm not handing you a blank check to write me out of the picture."

"Would a blank check work?"

His audacity took her breath. "Could you possibly be more of a jack—"

The scrape of a shoe on asphalt drew her attention to another approaching male. Gage. Great. Two headaches. "I'll talk to you tomorrow."

"There's nothing you can't say in front of Gage. He's like family."

The statement only irritated her more. "Unlike

me who actually *is* family. I admire your loyalty. To your friends at least."

"What's your price, Lauren?" Trent asked.

She wanted to kick the knucklehead in the kneecap, but she'd encountered and dealt with worse than him before without resorting to assault. "You can't buy me off, *big brother.* You've had our mother for thirtysomething years. It's my turn to spend a little time with her. Don't worry. I'll give her back."

"You've known her all your life."

A gurgle of disgust bubbled up her throat. She cut a look at Gage, who stood by Trent's side. "I see your spy has debriefed."

Gage frowned. "Lauren, our conversation wasn't confidential."

"Don't waste your breath, Faulkner. I knew where your loyalties lay before we ever set foot on an airplane together."

Trent squared his shoulders, trying to intimidate her by towering over her. Too bad it didn't work. "If you've known our mother all your life, why are we only now hearing about you?"

"Because apparently *our* parent wanted to keep us all in the dark. She never told me about you, either." She turned away then turned back. "Did you know my father was one of the founders of Hightower Aviation?"

The men's breath whistled in stereo.

Trent scowled—his usual expression around her. "I've heard no such claim."

"And neither had I until I started clearing out my father's old papers. Your father and mine were in the Air Force together. I found pictures. They started HAMC after they got out. They were scraping along, strapped for cash when our grandfather Bernard Waterman came on the scene and offered them money in return for one-third ownership. I'm not sure how our mother plays into the picture."

"I'll have to verify your story."

"Good luck with that. Jacqui's not talking." But why? And why had her father kept the secret? "Don't sweat it, boss. I'm not demanding a percentage of the stock. My father sold out to our mother while she was pregnant with me, and as far as I can tell he got a fair price. He took that money and started Falcon Air with my uncle Lou, who also used to work here."

Suspicion narrowed Trent's eyes. "Your uncle?"

"Oh, for pity's sake, relax. He isn't a blood relative. You won't have another relative crawling out of the woodwork, showing up and asking for a job."

Gage shoved his hands in his overcoat pockets. "Trent and I are going to have a drink. Do you want to join us and tell us more about this history of HAMC?"

Trent stiffened as if Gage's invitation had surprised him.

Obviously they'd decided to tag team her out of a job. She hit the remote to unlock her door, opened it and slung her bag inside. "Nice try, Faulkner. But I have to fly in the morning and any alcohol within twelve hours of flight time gets me fired. Company policy."

"Nice truck," Gage said behind her. "Big engine."

"For a girl, you mean? I need ten cylinders to tow airplanes around back home." The Dodge SRT Ram was her pride and joy and had been a true labor of love shared with the people she cared most about. It would also be the last project she, her father and Uncle Lou would work on together.

"Look, if you guys are through with the interrogation, I need some shut-eye. I've been here since four this morning, and I'm due back at the same time tomorrow for our flight to Lancaster."

Trent nodded. "Good night."

"Go ahead," Gage told him. "I'll catch up with you at the restaurant."

After a moment's hesitation Trent strolled toward his BMW, leaving her alone with Gage. "You don't trust me much, do you, Lauren?"

"I don't know you well enough to trust you."

"You have nothing to fear from me as long as you're not out to hurt the Hightowers."

Not believing him for one second, she climbed into her truck. "I'll keep that in mind."

He braced one hand on each side of her door and leaned into the opening, crowding her. She caught a whiff of his minty breath. Her mouth dried and her pulse quickened.

He stopped inches from her face. "Let's get one thing straight. I don't need Trent to pimp for me. If I ask you to dinner, it's because I don't like eating alone. I'm not expecting more. You're not my type."

"Good, because you're not mine, either." She fired the words back automatically. Just because she didn't want him didn't mean his rejection didn't sting.

He straightened, withdrawing from her personal space. "I'll see you in the morning."

He turned on his heel and headed toward a black SUV with long, purposeful strides.

What was Gage's type? The question popped into her head unexpectedly as she turned her key.

Doesn't matter. Forget it. Go home.

But she had a feeling that now that her curiosity had been stirred, she wasn't going to be able to forget it.

Three

Lauren shifted uneasily on the front doormat of the opulent Hightower home. A less-desperate woman would go home without making an already-bad day worse, but knowing Trent had dinner plans with Gage gave her a narrow window of opportunity to talk to her mother before he arrived home.

The door opened and Fritz the butler stood framed in the entryway. "Good evening, miss."

"Hi, Fritz."

"Madame is waiting for you in the salon." He

turned and led the way like a butler cliché from an old movie, British accent, black suit, stiff posture and all.

Lauren craned her neck, once again awed and a little intimidated by the soaring foyer with its priceless art collection and grand staircase. Her heels tapped on the marble tiles and the sound echoed off the walls, making her want to tiptoe. Honestly, the place was like a museum or a governor's mansion or something. How could anyone be comfortable here?

Fritz stepped aside and gestured to the open door with its fancy wood trim. "May I bring you anything? Wine? Coffee? Perhaps a light snack?"

"No, but thank you." How could she eat when every encounter with her mother was like an armed truce?

Fritz bowed and retreated, leaving Lauren once more with the surreal sense of being blown off course and landing on a foreign airstrip where you didn't know if the natives were friendly or hostile or even which language they'd speak.

The Hightower abode was hardly the kind of place you could kick your shoes off and wander around in your jammies.

"You've come straight from work." Her mother's voice pulled her attention back to the massive room. Jacqui sat in a chair by the fireplace looking almost regal in her black pantsuit, heels and diamonds. "The HAMC uniform looks good on you and makes me quite glad I insisted on skirts instead of pants for our female pilots."

"Um…yeah, thanks. I appreciate you letting me stop by on short notice."

"I'm always happy to see you, Lauren."

Oh, right. Jacqui emitted about as much warmth as an Alaskan winter. There was no shared hug, just a meaningless air kiss. They barely even touched. Her father or Uncle Lou would have swept Lauren up into a big lung-crushing, feet-lifted-off-the-ground hug after a long absence. But the Hightowers weren't the warm and fuzzy type.

"Come in and sit down."

Lauren perched on the edge of a brocade sofa with fancy fringe trim. How could she not have realized Jacqui was her mother sooner? They shared the same build and the same features, although her mother did something to brighten the mousy shade of her upswept hair and her makeup was always immaculate. Jacqui looked good, but Lauren wasn't into high maintenance. She'd stick with her naturally boring hair and soap, water and sunscreen regimen.

"I have some questions about my father."

Jacqui sniffed. "I can't talk about him yet. I miss him too much." Her emotion appeared genuine. But it had been two months—two months with a lot of meaningless chitchat, but no answers.

Lauren was beyond frustrated. "I miss him, too, Jacqui, but I need to understand his state of mind before the accident."

Jacqui rose and went to the wet bar to refill her glass instead of ringing for Fritz the way she had during Lauren's previous visits. "I can't pretend to know what your father was thinking."

"You were the last one to talk to him. Did he seem upset, distracted or depressed to you?"

Her mother faced her but didn't return to her seat. "Depressed? I don't know what you mean."

Lauren took a deep breath. She hadn't discussed the rumors with anyone other than her uncle. "A couple of his friends think the crash wasn't an accident. They claim Dad bragged that if he died, his life insurance policy would pay off Falcon Air's debts."

Jacqui stiffened and paled. She pressed a beringed, manicured hand to her chest. "No. No. Never. Kirk would never voluntarily leave me. Or you. From the moment I told him I'd conceived, you were his life. He planned everything around providing for you."

Emotion welled inside Lauren, tightening her chest. "I don't think he would have deliberately crashed, either. I mean, I can't believe I would have missed him being that upset. He was preoccupied those last few months, but I don't think he was unhappy." But had she missed something? "The life insurance company is refusing to pay the claim until they finish their investigation and rule out suicide."

"I'll give you whatever you need. Tell me how much."

Lauren shook her head. "I've told you before I don't want your money. I just want to know what you and my father discussed that last day before you left him *again*. That conversation could be a key to what happened."

Tears pooled in Jacqui's eyes. Was she faking it? "You believe I had something to do with his crash?"

"How can I know if you won't talk?"

"Lauren…I can't…discuss this."

"But—"

"I know you don't believe me, but I loved Kirk. He is the only man I ever loved, and knowing I'll never see him again—" Her voice broke. Her hand trembled as she set down her glass and covered her mouth.

Lauren hardened herself to the emotion. Jacqui was hiding something. The question was, what? "What about your husband?"

"That was an arranged marriage. My father promised to invest in Hightower Aviation if William married me."

"And you agreed?"

"I was a bit of a...difficult girl. My father wanted me to settle down. He threatened to cut me off without a cent if I didn't do as he ordered. William was quite a dashing pilot at the time. I thought I could grow to love him. I was wrong."

But she was still married to the guy. "Where did my father fit into this triangle?"

"William's only loves were flying and gambling. When my father died unexpectedly, I discovered my husband had gambled us into financial difficulty. I had to learn how to manage HAMC's assets because my husband was too busy having fun elsewhere. Your father helped me. Our...friendship soon became more. I knew it was wrong. But I fell in love with Kirk, and he with me."

Lauren shifted, not wanting to believe her father had knowingly slept with a married woman.

"When I became pregnant with you, your

father gave me an ultimatum. Leave William and come to him or we were over. But I couldn't. My father had written into his will that if I left my husband, I'd lose everything. My trust fund. My inheritance. My stock in Hightower Aviation. I had my other children to think of. I couldn't leave them to be raised by that—their father."

"You left me easily enough."

"William pressured me into giving you up. Kirk insisted on adopting you. I agreed, but only if I could visit you. Your father's stipulation was that we not tell you I was your mother. He didn't want you to feel rejected."

But Lauren had always wondered why her mother couldn't love her and didn't want her. "If you loved my father that much, how could you have been happy with only seeing him once a year?"

"That was all William would allow me. I lived for that week."

So had her father. Lauren had experienced a love-hate reaction with Jacqui's visits. On one hand while her mother was there, her father had been happier than she'd ever seen him, but every time Jacqui left he'd been devastated. And nothing Lauren had done had been enough to cheer him up.

She scanned the expensively decorated room. "Yes, it looks like you had a rough time. Living in the lap of luxury with servants at your beck and call when you weren't with Dad and I must have been difficult."

Jacqui cringed at the sarcasm in Lauren's voice. "I would have been with you if I could."

Lauren tried to work up sympathy and failed. Her mother had chosen financial security over a man who'd adored her and would have done anything for her. "So you don't think my father committed suicide?"

Again, Jacqui flinched. "Your father had too much to live for to harm himself. He had such plans, such high hopes."

Lauren wanted to believe her. But there was something fishy in the way Jacqui's gaze kept flitting around the room and never directly engaging with Lauren's.

The front door opened. Male voices bounced off the walls. Lauren stiffened. Gage and Trent. What had happened to their dinner plans? She looked at the archway, praying they'd pass by, but Trent's scowling face glared back at her.

"Mother, I didn't know you were expecting company." An arctic chill radiated from his voice.

"You know Lauren is always welcome here."

Gage said nothing, but his dark assessing eyes lasered in on Lauren. She had every intention of finding out what Jacqui was hiding, but she wouldn't get her answers tonight. She couldn't risk Trent overhearing the questionable circumstances of her father's death. The charter jet business was a small and competitive one. One word to the wrong people and Falcon would be grounded. Permanently.

Lauren rose. "I was just leaving. Good night, Jacqui. Gentlemen, I'll see you in the morning."

"Any news?" Lauren asked the moment her uncle answered the phone twenty minutes later.

She locked her apartment door and set her keys and bag on the nearby table.

"Nothing."

She'd been frustrated by her lack of progress with her mother and needed to talk to someone who understood. "Why is this taking so long? Daddy's been gone two months."

"Lauren, sweetie, your father's case may be number one to us, but it's not to the rest of the world. To them he was just another pilot in an experimental aircraft. He wasn't running from criminal charges or trafficking drugs or anything else that would make him a high priority."

"But Lou—"

"The crashes that have happened since his are higher profile. When are you coming home?"

She unpinned her hair, trying to relieve the slight headache Trent and Gage always gave her. "I don't know. Jacqui's still playing the grieving lover role. I'll try to call the investigators again tomorrow."

"No point. I called today to make sure they had your correct address. They promised the report would be couriered to you as soon as it's done. Just finish whatever it is you're trying to do and get home. I need you here. And I miss you, baby girl."

Her chest tightened. Lou had been a second father to her. Moving to Knoxville on the heels of her father's death was almost like losing both of them. "I miss you, too, Lou."

"Call the minute you get the report."

"I will. Keep your cell phone on."

"I'll try to remember."

She rolled her eyes. "Don't try. Just do it. Love you. I'll call again soon."

And hopefully, by the next time she called she'd have the answers they all needed to be able to get back to life as usual and focus on getting Falcon Air back into the black.

"She's done it again." Trent's angry voice barked through Gage's wireless cell phone earpiece late Wednesday afternoon.

"Who's done what?" Gage's grip tightened on the steering wheel of the sedan he'd rented.

"My mother withdrew almost two hundred thousand dollars from one of her accounts today."

Gage's breath whistled through his teeth. Jacqueline Hightower had always liked her expensive toys. "Has she been car shopping again?"

"I doubt there's a dealership on the island of Anguilla. That's where Mother is now. She flew out early this morning. I'll bet that little leech is connected. Why else would Lauren have been at my house last night? Is she with you now?"

Gage pinched the bridge of his nose, hoping to ward off the tension headache taking root between his eyes. The CEO he'd spent the day with had been difficult and defensive. In the end, Gage had refused the job and walked out.

Turning down work was still difficult for him. He wanted the security each job put in his investment account, but his time was short and the list of clients requesting his expertise was long enough to allow him to choose the ones who truly wanted his help and were ready to accept it rather than deal with the ones who fought his suggestions each step of the way as this one would have.

"No. I just left the job site. I'm on the way to the airport now."

"Tell Lauren to report to my office as soon as she's locked down the plane."

Gage scanned the dense fog outside the windows of his rental car. His headlights barely penetrated the near whiteout. "Check the forecast. Unless she's going to fly blind I don't think we'll be home tonight."

A moment later Trent's curse rang in his ears.

"Don't sweat it, Trent. This could work in your favor. The weather will keep your sister out of town overnight while you track the money trail. I'll use the time to see if I can find out anything relevant to your situation."

It wasn't as if he'd be befriending Lauren. He was simply protecting Trent's interest and digging for facts—something he did every day in his job.

Gage refused to stand by and let someone else's greed derail Trent's years of hard work. Loyalty to his friend wouldn't allow it.

* * *

Lauren shifted in the passenger seat of the rental car, glanced down at her HAMC uniform and then up at the restaurant looming out of the fog. *Not again.* Why did life keep throwing men who seemed determined to prove she couldn't fit into their world at her? It was probably a good thing her last relationship hadn't worked out. If she'd married Whit—not that he'd asked—she would have struggled against a lifetime of being a misfit. Ditto trying to fit into the Hightower clan.

"Can we go somewhere less…?"

Gage glanced her way as he pulled into the valet parking lane behind three other cars. "Less what?"

"Highfalutin. I realize you're accustomed to places like this, but I'm more interested in a filling meal than swanky presentation and having to worry about which fork to use."

No matter what her half brother ordered she should never have agreed to have dinner with Gage. But being grounded at a small rural airport by heavy fog had limited her options. Gage hadn't requested in-flight meals, so there hadn't been any food stashed on board, and the airport didn't have a restaurant. She hadn't wanted to waste money on a taxi.

An elegantly clad couple exited the brass-and-glass etched doors and headed for the valet stand, confirming her opinion. "I'm not dressed for this."

Gage inched the car forward. "What makes you think this is my kind of place?"

She flipped a wrist, indicating his tailored suit. He still looked as *GQ* fresh as he had when he'd met her at the terminal sixteen hours ago in the misty morning light. "You're buddies with Trent, which means you were probably born in a suit and carrying a silver spoon. Correction. You probably had a nanny on standby to carry it for you from the moment you took your first breath."

Gage's eyes crinkled with amusement. Lauren jerked back, her breath and heart hitching in tandem. *Wow.* The man was seriously gorgeous when he flashed those pearly whites.

Too bad he was taboo.

But even if he weren't, her life was too complicated for a relationship right now. Besides,

Gage had the money thing going, and, compliments of Whit, she'd sworn off rich guys forever. Their sense of entitlement and belief that less-fortunate people had been put on this planet for their use rubbed her the wrong way. Her new family only reinforced that point.

Gage's smile faded. "I wasn't born to money, Lauren. I earned everything I have. But I appreciate a good meal and superior service."

She searched his face in the glow of the dashboard lights. Could he possibly be telling the truth? If not, he lied flawlessly. "Your parents weren't loaded?"

"No."

"How did you go to that expensive university with Trent?"

The broad shoulder nearest her lifted. "Scholarships, financial aid and a job."

He pulled up to the valet station, put the car in Park, released his seat belt and reached for the door handle.

Lauren grabbed his arm, her fingers curling around big, firm bicep. His body heat seeped through his clothing and warmed her palm. She let go and laid her hand in her lap. "Gage, I'd feel more comfortable elsewhere."

He scanned her. "You look fine. No one will turn you away."

Dread curdled in her stomach. She wrinkled her nose and nodded to the couple climbing from the car in front of them. "Do the words *little black dress, heels* and *pearls* mean anything to you?"

He followed her gaze, refastened his safety belt and put the car in gear. "We'll head toward the hotel and see if we can find a restaurant on the way."

"That would be great. Thanks." After two hours of waiting to take off on the runway and being turned back when the airport ceased operation, they'd both been too hungry to check in to the hotel before dinner. Her instrument rating didn't count for beans when the airport shut down before she could get the wheels up. Smaller airports were great when a pilot wanted to avoid traffic, but the downside was some didn't operate when conditions were less than optimal.

Gage pulled out of the valet lane and drove out of the parking lot. "I heard you making a phone call earlier. Something about a bike trip tomorrow?"

He must have eavesdropped while he'd been arranging their hotel rooms. "I needed to let my landlord know I wouldn't be home. She'll relay the message to the neighbors who were meeting me tomorrow morning."

"Your landlord keeps tabs on you?"

"I'm renting the apartment over her garage." Wanting to end the personal questions, Lauren bailed out of the car the moment he parked, hustled for the sidewalk and waited for him to join her. The look he cut her as they entered the building let her know he was on to her.

"What kind of ride did you have planned?"

The smell of grilled fajitas and thick burgers made her mouth water and her stomach rumble. She hadn't had anything to eat since the sandwich she'd packed for lunch.

"I was going on a group motorcycle ride with

my neighbors. They're showing me the best of Knoxville on my days off. I was with them when Trent called me into the office to meet you."

He didn't speak again until after the hostess had seated them and departed. "Your neighbors are bikers?"

"Don't say it like it's a bad thing. They're great people. I found them through an online Harley chapter, and when I posted my plan to move to Knoxville they all but adopted me. One even hooked me up with my landlord. Her apartment is ten times better than any complex in the area and half the price. The day I pulled into her driveway my new friends were waiting to help me unpack."

"They were probably checking to see if you had anything worth stealing."

His words said a lot about the company he kept. "Not exactly a trusting soul, are you, Faulkner?"

"Where I came from if something wasn't nailed down, it was fair game."

"Not a nice neighborhood?"

He eyed her as if debating his words. "I spent a good part of my youth on welfare, and part of that living in my father's car."

Shock stole her breath. She didn't want to think of him as a poor, hungry kid or see an approachable side of him. She'd much rather believe he was a spoiled, stuck-up jerk like Trent, Brent and Beth, her three oldest half siblings. Only Nicole, the one closest to Lauren in age seemed to have any redeeming qualities. "I'm sorry, Gage. That's no way to live."

Regret tightened his mouth, as if he were sorry he'd revealed that bit of his past. "I'm not asking for sympathy. The point is you don't deserve anything you don't earn."

His hard tone let her know his barriers were up, and he didn't intend to give her any more peeks into his personal life.

"I agree, and I've worked hard for everything I have."

An expression of disbelief crossed his face.

The server arrived to take their orders. Once he left, Gage looked at her across the table. The

probing way he studied her made her uncomfortable. A speculative gleam entered his dark eyes.
"You said you grew up around an airport. Regardless of the city, that's not usually the best
section of town."

Another personal foray, but given what he'd
shared she decided it wouldn't hurt to respond
to this one. "We had a small, but comfortable
house near Daytona International. We weren't
high-class, but we weren't poor, either. I didn't
attend private schools, belong to a country club
or have servants, a pool, tennis court or any of
the other luxuries the Hightowers seem to think
they can't function without."

"Does it bother you that your mother's other
children had more than you?"

"No. If anything I'm appalled by their depen-
dence on others for even the simplest things.
Don't get me wrong. I'm used to people with
money. After all, they are the ones who charter
jets. But the Hightower's over-the-top lifestyle
is like something you'd see on TV. None of them
had jobs until after college. Even then, they were

hired by the family firm, so there's no chance of getting fired for poor performance."

He sipped his bourbon. "Don't you work for your father?"

He was really determined to see her in a bad light, wasn't he? "I didn't initially. I started with odd jobs for other pilots and owners around the airport. Sweeping hangars, washing and waxing planes and cars. My dad made it very clear that if I did sloppy work, it would reflect badly on him.

"Then from the day I turned sixteen until I was certified as a flight instructor I worked in food service. I realize asking 'Do you want fries with that?' isn't anything to brag about, but at least I learned how to earn and manage money and work with the public."

Despite his relaxed posture his alert eyes assessed her over the rim of his glass. "You didn't go to college, did you?"

"Trent has been sharing stuff from my personnel file again." The rat. "I have an associate's degree from community college, and—"

She bit her lip and studied her hands. She was working on a bachelor's degree from the University of Central Florida, but if her father's life insurance didn't pay up, she might not be able to afford to finish it. So close, and yet so far from attaining her goal. Getting her degree was more important now than ever. If Falcon Air failed, she'd have to find another employer, and the major airlines required a four-year degree.

And then there was Uncle Lou. At his age he'd have trouble finding another position, and he'd invested all his savings into Falcon. She might need to make enough to support both of them.

"And?" Gage prompted.

She wasn't whining to a stranger about her money problems—especially one who'd probably parrot her words to her half brother. Her situation would only reinforce her half sibling's opinion that she was here to take a bite out of their inheritance. Time to talk about someone else.

"You seem very familiar with traveling in the copilot seat."

Gage held her gaze long enough that she began to doubt he'd let her change the subject. Finally, he lifted one shoulder. "I used to fly with Trent."

Surprise made her sit up straighter. "Trent has his pilot's license? But he always uses a full crew when he travels. He never takes the controls."

She knew because she'd been cursed with him as a hypercritical passenger on her first dozen flights.

"He works en route."

"If he'd take the controls now and then, maybe he wouldn't be so uptight. I can't imagine being content to sit in the back and let someone else have all the fun."

Gage's eyes narrowed. "You could have a point. He used to love flying."

"You should mention that next time you report in."

The arrival of their salads kept him from replying. After the server left, Gage picked up his fork. "Tomorrow we'll rent a couple of motorcycles from the Harley dealership and tour the area."

Excitement inflated inside her like a balloon. She popped it. Was this like demanding her presence at dinner? She had to comply? "I don't want to spend the cash."

"I'll cover it."

"Renting requires a motorcycle endorsement on your license."

"I haven't ridden in years, but I have it."

She studied him. Gage, with his perfectly fitting suits and immaculate haircut, looked far too sophisticated and uptight to climb on the back of a bike and roar down the roads with the wind whipping at his clothes. Not that there weren't thousands of executives who rode motorcycles, but Gage had an ever-present tension in him that hinted he never loosened up. "I don't believe you."

He extracted his license from his wallet and offered it to her. "I couldn't afford a car in college. I rode an old bike."

She snatched the small card from his hand. Yep. He had the endorsement. She noted his age, thirty-five, then checked his face. The brackets beside his mouth and the groove in his forehead made him look older.

She was about to pass his license back when his address caught her attention. "I know this address. The neighborhood is near my apartment and…not at all ritzy."

"I don't believe in wasting money on frivolous things."

"Like private jets?" The sarcastic quip was out of her mouth before she could stop it. Whoops.

Gage's eyebrows descended. He took the license from her and tucked it into his wallet. "Two of my associates are on parental leave. I'm covering my position in addition to theirs. I'm spending a lot of time in the air, but thanks to HAMC, a lot more time on the job and less time waiting in airport security lines. If I'd been flying commercial today, I would have either missed my flight or had to leave before the job was completed and return to finish my assessment. Either way, that would have cost me money. In the long run flying privately is more efficient since my time and expertise is what people purchase."

She grimaced. "Sorry. I guess I have a bit of a chip on my shoulder. I can't get used to the Hightowers' conspicuous consumption. They throw away a lot of money on extravagant stuff."

"And you don't?"

"I'm pretty thrifty."

His disbelieving chuckle sent a shiver of awareness through her. "Lauren, you own a motorcycle, a truck and an airplane—all three high-performance, pricy models."

Trent again. She smothered a growl of frustration. "Big brother has been talking. Not that it's any of your business, but for the record, I bought my truck from a salvage yard. Dad, Lou and I rebuilt her together. It gets poor gas mileage, but I need it for work, so I started looking for something more economical to drive.

"I got my motorcycle at half price by trading the owner for flying lessons. Consider it sweat equity. My airplane was a similar too-good-to-be-true bargain. The owner was having financial difficulties and needed to unload her quickly. He asked around at the airport to see if anyone might be interested in buying it. My father over-heard him and told me. I took out a business loan because I make most of my living with that Cirrus. It's not a toy. It's my office."

A slow smile started in his eyes and spread to his mouth. The combo of gleaming dark eyes and white teeth stole her breath. She leaned back in her chair, putting as much distance between them as possible without actually leaving the table. The odd lightness in her tummy had better be hunger. She couldn't afford for it to be anything else.

"You're a mass of contradictions, Lauren Lynch. I apologize for jumping to conclusions."

In that moment she actually liked him.

He's the enemy, your half brother's spy and wealthy. Three strikes.

The waiter set their meals on the table and departed, but the interruption was enough to allow suspicion to overtake Lauren's brain. Why was Gage suddenly being so warm and ap-proachable if not to set her up and take her down? He and her brother were in cahoots.

"It won't work, Gage."

"What's that?" he asked, looking up from his thick salmon steak.

"Charming me."

One dark eyebrow hiked. "Excuse me?"

"I'm on to the scheme you and Trent have cooked up. I've been burned by one of you rich guys before, and I learned my lesson. I don't care how attractive you are, I won't—"

"You find me attractive?" His eyes crinkled deliciously and a miniature stunt plane did a loop-de-loop in her midsection.

She frowned at him and ignored his question. "I will not violate HAMC policies by getting personally involved with you. So stop smiling and flirting."

"I'm not flirting."

"Oh, please. Don't bat your lashes at me. I'm not buying that innocent act. And what do you call renting motorcycles and spending the day playing tourist together if you're not trying to get me to let down my guard?"

His expression turned serious. "If I hadn't been

late arriving at the airport, we'd have taken off before the fog descended, and you'd be home by now. My overtime cost you your day off. The motorcycle ride is to replace the one I took from you."

Speechless and more than a little suspicious, she stared into his dark eyes, searching for the truth. That sounded fair-minded and almost *nice.* She didn't want him to be nice. She wanted him to be a conceited prick. Like Trent.

But she wasn't dumb enough to look a gift horse in the mouth. She'd always wanted to see the Dutch Amish countryside, and her father had always said, "Take a little of each place you visit home with you." She'd just have to be careful and not fall for Gage's handsome face, his devastating grin or let his sneaky charm worm information out of her that she wasn't willing to share. Of course, that wasn't anything she couldn't handle. Not after the lesson Whit had taught her.

"Okay, Faulkner, you're on. But I'm in charge. Road rules state the most experienced rider leads. That's me. If you can't handle following, speak up now."

One corner of his mouth curled upward. "I can handle anything you can dish out and then some, Lynch. Bring it on."

Lauren's bike engine wasn't the only thing revving as Gage strode across the parking lot toward her.

A muscle-hugging black leather jacket accentuated his broad shoulders and lean torso. Matching chaps framed the denim covering the male package behind the fly of his jeans like a Look Here sign. He paused beside his motorcycle to don his black helmet and pull on his gloves, then he mounted the machine.

She visually traced the line of his straight back, his long legs and the booted feet he'd planted squarely on the asphalt. She told herself she was assessing his form and therefore his skill level, but knew she lied.

He looked good straddling a Harley. Good and hot.

And that was *baaaad*. For her peace of mind, anyway.

Luckily, she'd ridden her motorcycle to work yesterday, and had stowed her riding gear on the plane. Not so Gage. He wore "tags barely off" new everything from the skivvies out— assuming he wore underwear. The biker attire suited him as well as his tailored suit had, maybe better. And thank God he had the intelligence to wear a helmet even though Pennsylvania law didn't require one.

With concentrated effort she forced her attention away from the man beside her to the GPS on the rental rumbling between her legs. After double-checking the route the salesperson had suggested, she heeled up her kickstand.

Gage's gaze scraped her from head to toe. Appreciation replaced the anticipation sparkling in his eyes. Her breath caught and suddenly her neck warmer felt tighter and itchier than a too-small turtleneck sweater. She tugged the stretchy fleece away from her skin and inhaled a lungful of cool air.

He zipped his jacket and flipped down his visor then started his bike and twisted the throttle, making the engine roar. His thigh muscles bunched as he balanced the heavy weight of the bike, making her think of other activities that caused those same muscles to flex. Not something she needed to think about if she wanted to be steady on her wheels.

She cleared her throat. "Ready?"

"Ready." His voice was strong and sure.

Oh, yeah, he'd ridden before and his confidence in his ability to control the powerful motorcycle came through loud and clear.

Damn. Confidence looked good on him. Good and sexy.

Her palms moistened in her gloves and heat filled her jacket and helmet despite the nip in the autumn air. A chilly ride was exactly what she needed to clear her head. A little hypothermia would fix what ailed her. "Follow my lead and watch for my hand signals."

"Just ride, Lauren. I've got your back."

She lowered her visor, put the bike in gear and pulled out of the parking lot. She'd bet her Harley Gage would rather lead than follow, but she'd dealt with hardheaded students before. She knew when to dig in and when to be flexible. Allowing shenanigans could get someone hurt or killed. And one death in the family was all Falcon Air could handle.

Four

Gage's pulse pounded in his ears, and adrenaline pulsed through his veins, energizing his muscles and sharpening his senses. Wind pummeled his leather jacket and whistled through the vents on his full-face helmet.

Ahead of him, Lauren leaned into a curve, her body moving as one with the machine beneath her. He did the same, savoring the power and responsiveness of the well-balanced Harley. It had taken almost an hour for the feel for riding to return, and for him to get comfortable on the bike. As if Lauren had anticipated that, she'd taken it easy on him for the first leg of their trip. Now she pushed him, going a little faster and taking more challenging routes. She leaned farther into each curve.

He hadn't realized how much he'd missed cutting through the air like a missile. He caught himself grinning inside his helmet and surprise sobered him.

In college he'd ridden a motorcycle due to necessity, not for pleasure, and his inability to afford a car had been an embarrassment and an obstacle to overcome. When he'd sold that old clunker he'd sworn he'd never have another motorcycle. Today's outing made him rethink that decision.

He focused on the curve of Lauren's leather-clad butt. Who was this woman in front of him? Her pleasure in riding the winding roads through the rolling farmlands and roaring through the covered bridges and past silos, horse-drawn buggies, frolicking goats and stacks of hay bales couldn't be more obvious or more contagious. The simple things she pointed out contradicted

Trent's certainty that Lauren was a mercenary bitch out to tap the Hightower keg and drain it dry.

In fact, everything Gage had learned about her to this point went against Trent's theory, but Trent had always been a shrewd judge of character. He'd been the only one to warn Gage that Angela was lying about agreeing to forgo children and all she wanted was a meal ticket.

Too bad Gage hadn't been smart enough to listen to his friend and dump Angela instead of marrying her. He'd been blinded by lust and love and bought Angela's pretty little lie that he was all she'd ever need. A year later when he'd stood firm on the no-children issue she'd pleaded and pouted then threatened and finally left him, taking a chunk of his net worth with her in the divorce settlement. If he'd put the no-kids clause in writing, she wouldn't have been able to use it against him. He shook off the negative memory of his ex-wife.

Could Trent be wrong about Lauren? Doubtful. If anything, Gage wasn't seeing clearly due to his attraction to Lauren.

Lauren signaled a left turn and pulled into a rural diner parking lot. Gage geared down and followed her, stopping beside her and killing his engine. The absolute silence of the countryside soaked into him.

She flipped up her visor. "Let's eat before we head back."

"Sounds good." Dismounting, he peeled off his gloves and reached up to remove his helmet. Something felt different. He rolled his shoulders trying to pinpoint the change and discovered the persistent knots that had cramped his neck and upper back for the past year had vanished.

He unzipped his jacket. Cold air bit his hands and cheeks. But it felt good. *He* felt good, and eager for the next leg of the journey. His disappointment over yesterday's wasted hours had vanished.

How long had it been since he'd taken a day off? He couldn't remember. He used to vacation with Trent a couple of times a year, but lately both of them had been too busy to even make their monthly dinners.

After removing her helmet, Lauren turned in

a slow circle, scanning the brown patchwork fields surrounding them and finger-combing the tangles from her hair. "Isn't it beautiful?"

She was beautiful. The defensive edge she usually wore had vanished. Her cheeks were flushed and her teal eyes sparkled with joy, vitality and excitement—all of the things that had been lacking from his life lately. If he could have absorbed her energy into his being at that moment, he would have. The temptation to try pulled at him, moving him forward until the toes of their boots touched.

He lifted a hand and cupped her cheek. Her widened gaze bounced to his. Awareness edged out exuberance, expanding her pupils. She shivered.

Her scent, a combination of her leather riding apparel, the outdoors and a trace of flowers invaded his nostrils and sank heavily to his groin.

Gage's eyes focused on her moist, pink mouth. He told himself to back away. Given Trent's suspicions, acting on this chemistry was a bad idea. Instead, he leaned forward. Lauren's head tilted back. Her lips parted and her gold-tipped lashes descended. A puff of her warm breath teased his chin, and his heart hammered against his ribs.

Contact with her lips—soft, damp lips—zapped him like static electricity, but the spark was far from superficial. He felt it deep in his gut. Hell, the current charged through all his extremities. Eager for more of her taste, he opened his mouth and stroked her bottom lip with his tongue. She tasted of cherry Chap Stick lip balm and…Lauren.

She sighed into his mouth, and her breasts nudged his chest. He cupped her waist, stroked her back, then the tight curve of her leather-clad bottom to pull her closer.

She stiffened. Her eyes flew open, meeting his gaze over their joined mouths. She planted her palms on his chest and shoved, nearly knocking him off his feet.

Wiping her mouth, she backed away. "Nice try, Faulkner. But you're not going to cost me this job."

A sharp gust of wind punctuated her statement and cooled the embers she'd ignited. Gage studied her flushed face.

Who was the real Lauren Lynch? The simple woman who wore Chap Stick and enjoyed the Amish countryside? Or the one out for everything she could siphon from her rich relatives? With two hundred grand unaccounted for, Gage couldn't be too careful.

For Trent's sake, he would find out Lauren's objectives. It was the least he could do to repay his debt.

But sleeping with the enemy wasn't part of the plan.

No matter how good she tasted.

The combination of driving rain, a chilly forty degrees and twenty-mile-per-hour crosswinds had added a little extra excitement to Lauren's Thursday-night landing in Knoxville. Those same conditions were going to make her motorcycle ride home from the airport miserable.

She hadn't packed her rain suit when she'd left for work yesterday morning because the cold front hadn't been predicted to dip this far south. Maybe the Fates were giving her the cold shower she deserved for aborting her common sense this afternoon and kissing her brother's spy.

Her pulse skipped just thinking about the firm possession of Gage's mouth, his warm lips and the heat of his hands on her behind. She blew out a slow breath and tried to shake off the arousal prickling her skin like a coarse wool blanket.

Gage would not sneak beyond her fences again. Not today or any other day. But his boyish grin when he'd climbed off that Harley Night Rod had knocked reason right out of her head. The man took himself too seriously. The fact that he'd seemed surprised to have enjoyed the ride had doubled the knee-weakening power of his blinding smile, and those glittering golden-brown eyes had hit her harder than a triple shot of Goldschlager.

Gage Faulkner was dangerous. Probably more so than Whit had been because she'd known what her ex-lover wanted from the moment he'd swept her off her feet with that first fancy dinner. Gage was sneakier and more devious because while the attraction crackled between them, so did the antagonism. But she knew his game plan now. Charm her. Disarm her. Get her fired.

In her logbook, once a fool didn't mean always a fool. She knew better than to mistake herself for Cinderella again. She'd learned the hard way there was no happily ever after for a rich man and a working-class woman. The wealthy took what they wanted short-term then moved on to a more suitable mate for the long haul, one who had connections and social graces. Like the congress-man's debutante daughter Whit had married.

That meant Lauren had to get rid of Gage. But how?

She locked the plane then hunched her shoul-ders and sprinted through the downpour toward the terminal a hundred yards away. She'd dropped Gage off closer to the building where an attendant had been waiting with an umbrella to escort him inside, then she'd taxied the Mustang to her assigned spot on the tarmac.

Cold droplets slipped down the back of her neck, soaked through her uniform and spattered her legs beneath her skirt as she splashed across the concrete. She shook off what moisture she could and debated calling a taxi, but she wanted to send Uncle Lou as much money as she could to cover her father's—now her—share of the expenses, and the ride to her apartment on the other side of town would run at least fifty bucks. The equivalent of a week's worth of groceries.

Drenched and shivering, she opened the door. Inviting heated air welcomed her, but the sight of Gage waiting in the lobby stopped her on the threshold. She'd taken her time locking down the plane hoping he'd be long gone before she came inside.

"Is there a problem?" she asked.

"Park your Harley in the hangar. I'm giving you a ride home."

She opened her mouth to refuse what sounded more like an order than an offer. Other than flying around the storm, the flight home had been calm and enjoyable since, for once, Gage had buckled up in the passenger cabin where he belonged. The last thing she wanted was more time with him. Time to rehash that misbegotten kiss, time to smell his cologne and feel his presence and get her muscles all kinked up again with knots of tension.

But her daddy hadn't raised a fool. She'd rather be warm and dry than wet and proud. "Thanks. Let me turn over the flight log."

"I'll get the car and wait outside."

All too soon she'd handed over the report on the airplane's performance, secured her bike and stood beside the black Chevy SUV Gage had pulled beneath the covered drop-off area in front of HAMC's private departure lounge.

He opened her door. Their fingers touched as he took her flight bag from her, jarring her heart into an erratic beat and almost making her miss her footing as she climbed into the front seat. His steadying hand on her elbow didn't help her co-ordination any.

The big, powerful vehicle suited him, and the interior smelled like a combination of his cologne and leather upholstery. He strapped in beside her. Maybe she could convince him to talk to Trent about reassigning her on the way home. But within minutes the nasty weather combined with rush hour traffic changed her mind. She'd let Gage focus on getting them to her place without incident.

Water streamed down the windows, isolating them from the rest of the world. Intense concentration furrowed his forehead and stiffened his shoulders. She caught herself contrasting his hard, chiseled jaw with the relaxed and easy smile he'd worn when he'd climbed off the Harley.

Her gaze drifted to his thick dark hair. The neatly combed strands had gotten damp when he'd gone after his car, and the moisture gave the ends a slight curl. He looked more approachable with disheveled helmet hair. He'd probably look even better with bedhead.

The thought made her wince. Oh yeah, she had to get rid of him before she did something stupid. Like risk her job by kissing him again...or worse.

She'd never been a slave to desire before, had never been one of those silly, giggly girls she'd overheard on campus who couldn't wait until spring break to get wild, and she had no intention of getting goofy now. Not that she'd had that many opportunities to get stupid over a guy. But Whit had gotten to her. He'd slipped past her defenses and made her believe for a few short months that she could be more than a jet jockey.

Dumb. Dumb. Dumb. Besides, you love being a pilot.

She squinted and leaned forward to see through the windshield. Darkness and oncoming headlights combined with a fog building inside the car created an awful glare.

She reached for the defrost button and her hand collided with Gage's as he did the same thing. She jerked away, and let him adjust his own controls while she tried to quiet the buzz working through her system like a shorted-out wire.

"Take the next exit then the second right. It's the third house on the left."

He followed her instructions, pulled up to the garage and turned off the engine. Lauren jumped from the car and opened the back door to retrieve her bag. She turned and startled when she saw Gage standing beside her.

He clamped steadying hands on her upper arms.

"Sorry." She pulled free, but the feel of his hands remained after he'd moved out of her personal space. "Thanks for the ride."

"I'm coming up."

"Why?" A chilly raindrop slid down her cheek.

"You didn't leave on any lights."

Something inside her went mushy. She wasn't used to men other than her dad and Lou looking out for her. "I'll be fine."

"I'll see you inside." His inflexible tone warned her arguing would be a waste of time, and she wasn't really interested in getting soaked to prove a point.

Resigned, she led the way up the steep, shadowed stairs and unlocked her door. Stepping inside, she flicked on a glass lamp filled with seashells she and her father had collected on the Florida beaches. Seeing the lamp reminded her why she was here and why she couldn't let Gage blow this gig for her prematurely.

"See. Everything's good. I told you, it's a safe neighborhood. Not all bikers are roughneck gang members."

Gage moved forward out of the rain pounding the landing outside her door and forcing her deeper into her living room. He closed the door as his gaze raked over her belongings as if cataloging and valuing each item. "Nice."

A snort of disbelief escaped before she could stop it. The two-room apartment wasn't big or luxurious, but it was clean and comfortable, and her landlord, a widow, was a sweetie. Lauren had brought only the essential furniture with her since she'd known she wouldn't be staying long, and much to her mother's disgust there wasn't a designer anything anywhere in sight.

Jacqui kept offering to buy Lauren gifts or loan her money, but Lauren was equally determined to refuse. If her mother had wanted to show her affection, then she should have tried being a parent over the past twenty-five years instead of trying to buy Lauren's love now. The fact that

Jacqui had chosen to be a mother to her other children chafed.

Lauren shrugged off the wasted emotion. "The apartment serves its purpose."

"Good night, then."

She glanced at the lamp again and gathered her courage. "Gage."

His dark eyes found hers.

"You need to request another pilot."

A pleat formed between his leveled eyebrows. "Why?"

"Because what happened today can't happen again."

He folded his arms and squared his stance. "It won't."

And yet even as he said the words, his gaze dropped to her lips—lips which tingled in response to his expanding pupils.

"Please ask. Trent won't listen to me."

"And in this case, neither will I. You're mine for the duration of this contract, Lauren. Deal with it." He turned and left, his footsteps pounding down the wooden stair treads.

Lauren groaned in frustration and shut the door.

Nothing good would come of this. Of that she was certain.

She should have called in sick, Lauren decided as she stepped from the plane onto the tarmac.

She'd been tempted to play hooky from work even though she felt perfectly well. But she'd never skipped out on work before, and she wasn't going to let her half brother and his cohort drive her into developing bad habits now.

At any other time the assignment she'd picked up this morning would have filled her with excitement. Three days in San Francisco. Throw in the opportunity to fly a new-to-her model jet, and she was almost in heaven.

Except the fates weren't finished conspiring against her.

She swept a regretful glance over the Sino Swearingen SJ30-2. A sweet, hot little number with a peach of a cockpit. And unless she could find an available mechanic with fast diagnostic skills, she probably wouldn't get to fly her. She expelled a long, disappointed breath. Bummer.

The long layover in San Francisco meant she should have time to finish her economics paper and sightsee, but for that to happen she had to get a different airplane or get the radio fixed.

The terminal door opened as she approached and one of her current headaches stepped out— thirty minutes ahead of his ETA.

Gage's gaze ran over her, taking in her fitted black uniform jacket, pencil skirt and low heels. She'd never considered the HAMC uniform sexy, but the way he looked at her kicked her pulse up a notch. His attention settled on her mouth, and she could feel yesterday's kiss all over again. Her stomach hit turbulence. Wasn't it bad enough that she'd dreamed about that kiss last night? Repeatedly.

She mashed her lips together and snapped to attention, trying to rein in her inappropriate response. "Good morning, Mr. Faul—" His shoulders stiffened and his eyes darkened with anger. "Gage," she corrected quickly. So much for reestablishing proper protocol between them. "You're early. I still have a few things to take care of. Why don't you wait in the lounge and have a cup of coffee and maybe some breakfast?"

HAMC always put out a continental breakfast for its clients.

If she was lucky, he'd stay behind the bulkhead again today. Passengers, especially this one, belonged in the passenger cabin. She didn't want Gage in the copilot seat and didn't want to have to talk to him and edit every word that came out of her mouth.

"I've already had breakfast." His dark gaze shot beyond her to the aircraft then returned to her. "Is there a problem?"

"The Internet connection is down on the jet. It's probably just a loose wire in the transmitter. I'll get a mechanic to check it out. If it can't be fixed, I'll request another plane. Our Mustang is in for routine service today."

His jaw set in that stubborn angle she'd come to recognize didn't bode well for her. "I won't need the Internet on this trip."

But she would. Her paper was due by eight Monday morning. She still had to verify some research, do a final edit and submit her work to the professor via e-mail. Without the Internet she couldn't do any of those, and she didn't know where they'd be staying or if their hotel had service. She also needed to check in with her mother, who'd suddenly decided to play hard-to-get by taking a trip to the Caribbean.

Playing cat and mouse with Jacqui was getting tiresome. After two months of trying to get answers Lauren still had nothing. She was beginning to think her mother was avoiding her.

"It won't take long." She stepped forward to cut around Gage and enter the building, but he didn't move out of her way. She jerked to a halt, her shoulder touching his. A static shock skipped up her nerve endings, and his cologne invaded her senses before she could back away.

"Did everything else check out?" The minty smell of his breath caressed her face. His jaw gleamed from a recent shave.

"Yes, but—"

"And we both know you're thorough in your preflight check."

"Well, yes, but—"

"Let's stick with what we have. I'm short on time. Trent assures me this aircraft can go the distance without stopping to refuel, and it can land at the smaller airfield we're targeting."

"Yes, but—"

"Lauren, I don't have time for this." He caught her elbow and turned her toward the jet. The heat of his touch penetrated her suit jacket and kicked up a crosswind of sensation, but his high-handedness made her dig in her heels.

"Gage, I'd rather have a fully functional plane. We're early, and we'll make good ti—"

"If this one isn't unsafe—and I can't believe it is since it's your brother's personal aircraft—then let's go." He urged her toward the jet.

She planted her feet. "Gage—"

"Call it in, Lauren. Get it fixed on the other end." He pivoted and strode toward the jet without her.

She wanted to argue, to insist, to bash her head against the fuselage. But she couldn't. Her time was his time. HAMC wasn't paying her to do schoolwork. They were paying her to be a pilot at the client's disposal. They didn't care if she didn't get her degree and couldn't get another job.

The customer is always right unless safety is an issue.

Her father's words echoed in her head once again, reminding her why she was here. She sucked up her irritation and followed Gage to the aircraft, determined to get through the next three days without jeopardizing her job or her education.

Finding a hotel without Internet access in a metropolitan area like San Francisco had been a challenge, but Gage had succeeded—just as he'd succeeded in getting Trent to disable the Internet connection on the plane to keep Lauren from contacting her mother.

Encore, Please, the small bed-and-breakfast hotel in The Haight district of San Francisco had come highly recommended by a former client. It had no pool, no gym, no business center and no Internet—nothing like Gage's usual choice of accommodation. But he had to admit, despite the lack of amenities, the place had a certain charm.

If the property had belonged to him he would have toned down the girlie paint job in shades of lavender, purple and raspberry and eliminated some of the elaborate gingerbread trim and busy spindled railings. Otherwise the Victorian row house appeared to be a valuable, attractive and well-maintained piece of property in keeping with the surrounding homes and businesses.

A guest interested in relaxing would enjoy the postcard-worthy views from each window. But Gage didn't have time to unwind when he was doing the work of three consultants.

"Refill your glass, hon?" Esmé, the proprietress asked. "Another shrimp? Another stuffed mushroom?"

"No, thank you. It's all very good. But if you want me to have room for the delicious-smelling dinner you have prepared, I need to stop." There had been a time when he never refused food because he never knew when his next meal might be. But those days had passed.

When he'd returned from the job site he hadn't been interested in chatting with Esmé, a retired soap opera star with a dramatic flair, or Leon, her sixtysomething-year-old boyfriend, but the couple had somehow managed to bulldoze him onto the front porch and into a white wooden rocking chair and ply him with appetizers and Leon's homemade wine. They'd also put him through a thirty-minute inquisition worthy of the FBI with such subtlety that anyone who didn't dig for details for a living would never have recognized the interrogation. If his evasiveness frustrated them, they never let on. And they never let up.

He couldn't imagine Esmé making a profit running the B and B with the superior quality and high-end food she prepared for her few guests. But then Esmé probably didn't need money. She wore enough expensive jewelry to pay off a substantial mortgage and then some. For her sake, he hoped the gems were heavily insured.

But her finances were not his problem. He had papers to review and accounts to study for the company that had paid for his services, and he needed to locate Lauren. According to the couple, she'd left soon after they'd checked in this morning. Where in the hell had she gone?

"There's our girl now," Leon said.

Gage's abdomen tightened even before he looked in the direction his host indicated and spotted Lauren cresting the hill. A breeze lifted her straight hair away from her face. The setting sun streaked the strands with a copperish hue. Her jeans and zipped-up jacket outlined her slender shape. She paused, shifting her bag on her shoulder then turned toward Golden Gate Park as if soaking up the view one last time before retiring for the evening. Her jeans hugged her backside as faithfully as her leather riding pants had, but had interesting faded spots on each lower cheek. His body reacted predictably, given his recent all-work-and-no-play stint.

Why couldn't he get Lauren out of his head? The memory of that damned kiss and the feel of her pressed against him had disrupted his concentration all day, which was the reason he'd been forced to bring a case of files back to the B and B to work on tonight.

She pivoted and resumed walking toward the house. Where had she been all day?

She must have spotted the wildly waving Esmé because Lauren lifted a hand to wave. He knew the exact second she spotted him because her steps and hand faltered, and her blinding smile dimmed. Her fingers curled and her arm lowered. Even her stride changed from light and bouncy to laborious, as if she were slogging the last hundred feet uphill through knee-deep mud. Her obviously negative reaction nicked him, but he brushed it off. He didn't want to be her friend. Or her lover.

He might admire her confidence, competence and intelligence, but those were merely skills that made her a good pilot and a decent employee for Trent. Without trust none of those attributes mattered.

She climbed the stairs and both Esmé and

Leon jumped up to greet her like a grandchild they hadn't seen in months.

Esmé hooked an arm through Lauren's and all but dragged her to the rocking chair beside Gage's. "Did you find the Wi-Fi café and get your paper done?"

"I did. Your directions were excellent. My paper is finished and e-mailed to my instructor days early."

She'd been online again? "What paper?"

Lauren bit her lip and shifted on her feet. "I have an economics paper due Monday morning."

"You're taking a class?"

She hesitated as if debating answering…or making up one. "Yes. Online through the University of Central Florida. You didn't need me, did you? You could have called my cell phone."

Her face looked honest enough, but his goal of keeping her offline had failed. He'd need a new strategy for tomorrow. "No. I didn't need you."

Leon took her bag and pressed a glass of wine into Lauren's hand. "Try this. It's my latest batch of vino."

She smiled her thanks and the old man beamed.

"Why are you taking classes?" Gage asked, recapturing her attention.

"I'm working toward a four-year bachelor's degree in business administration. In this economic climate it's always good to have a backup plan."

Add ambitious to her list of assets. But was she the type to take shortcuts and use others for personal gain? Something didn't add up. The discrepancy between what Trent believed and what Gage saw was too great. Good thing Gage enjoyed solving puzzles because Lauren was a complicated one.

Esmé patted Lauren's shoulder. "Smart girl. And what about your mother? Were you able to reach her? Did she give you what you needed?"

Lauren hid a frown behind her glass as she sipped her wine and eased into the chair. If he hadn't been watching her closely, he would have missed her slight grimace. So she wasn't a fan of wine. But she smiled at her host and nodded her head as if she loved the subpar stuff rather than hurt Leon's feelings. "It's good."

That was an outright lie, but he could hardly blame her since he'd uttered the same one before she'd arrived. The wine had a distinctly metallic taste.

She tucked one foot beneath her in the chair. "I reached Mom, but she couldn't talk. She claimed she had to be somewhere. I'll try again tomorrow."

The hell she would. A sting of curses silently reverberated through Gage's head. Cutting Lauren off from the Internet had failed, and so had keeping her from contacting her mother.

"What do you need from your mother?" he asked.

She blinked at his unintentionally harsh tone and glanced away. "Answers."

He recognized evasion when he saw it. He'd mastered that particular skill. "What kind of answers?"

Lauren's teal gaze met his again. "She chose not to be my mother for twenty-five years. It would be nice to know why she changed her mind now."

That wasn't all. He could tell by her guarded expression that she was hiding something. What? And how could he uncover her secrets?

"You told me she'd always been a part of your life."

"Not as a parent. She was my father's…friend. She flew in once a year around my birthday and stayed for a week, but she spent most of her time with my father. I didn't mind, because during her stay he was always happier than at any other time of the year. He loved her. Too bad she didn't feel the same."

There was an edge in Lauren's voice that he couldn't quite decipher. She studied the burgundy liquid in her glass then looked up at him through narrowed eyes. "I talked to the mechanic this afternoon. Someone removed the fuse from the receiver that provides Internet access on the plane. It wasn't blown or broken. It was taken. Why would anyone do that?"

"Good question." And one he had no intention of answering since the action had been taken at his request.

Five

The city of San Francisco was waiting and Lauren was eager to hit the sidewalks and explore.

Trying to shake off the lingering tiredness her shower hadn't completely banished, she tightened the belt of the fluffy short white robe the B and B provided and stowed her toiletry items in her bag. She'd slept until six this morning, which was late for her because she usually had to be in the air by then, and given the time difference, she should have been up hours ago.

She blamed her sluggishness on all the tossing and turning she'd done last night. Her bedroom shared a wall with Gage's, and he must have stayed up late. She'd heard him moving around as if he were pacing, and a couple of times his deep voice had carried through the wall behind her headboard. Who had he been talking to at that time of night?

She opened the bathroom door and shuffled across the landing. Gage's bedroom door opened before she reached her room, and he stepped into the hall. Her muscles locked up. She'd forgotten their single rooms shared a hall bathroom.

Against her will she drank in his mussed hair, sleepy brown eyes, beard-shadowed jaw and broad, bare-chested, seriously well-developed body. The man worked out. Shoulders, biceps, pecs and abs like that didn't happen by accident.

Black trousers, probably from yesterday's suit, rode low on his hips, transecting a dark line of hair that descended from between his nipples to below his navel. His big feet were bare, his toes long and straight. Like her, he held a toiletry bag.

He belonged on a sexy Corporate Hotties pin-up calendar. Her pulse *whumped* in her ears like helicopter blades, and she couldn't seem to suck enough air into her lungs. It took a substantial effort to uncurl her toes. "G-good morning."

His eyes sharpened on her face then slowly descended to the plunging neckline of the wraparound robe and on to her bare legs and feet. Other than the slight expansion of his pupils, his expression gave nothing away. A guy with his money was probably used to models and beauty queens rather than tomboys who wore jeans and no makeup. Not that she cared.

"Morning." The sleep-roughened voice rasped over her, making the fine hairs on her arms rise.

Conscious of her wet hair, freshly scrubbed face and near nakedness, she clutched her travel bag to her chest. "I'm, uh…done. The bathroom's all yours."

To get to the bathroom he had to pass close by her. She caught a faint whiff of his cologne as the air stirred, but mostly she smelled Gage— slightly musky male. The close confines of a cockpit made someone's scent easily identifiable. Arousal flushed her skin and tightened her nipples, leaving her hot and bothered and wanting to shed the heavy robe. But that would have to wait until she'd shut the door behind her.

"Excuse me." She darted across the hall, not relaxing until she'd closed and locked the wooden panel between them. Knees weak, she sagged against the hard surface.

Why him? Why did Gage Faulkner agitate every feminine particle in her being into a whirlwind of certain disaster? It wasn't fair that the one guy she least wanted to be attracted to would affect her so strongly. But that didn't mean she'd be stupid and act on the bad mojo.

She listened for sounds from the hall while she hastily pulled on jeans and layered a sweater over her T-shirt then shoved her feet into sneakers. After she heard Gage reenter his room, she grabbed her jacket, wallet and computer backpack and jogged down the stairs.

Esmé met her in the foyer. "Good morning, dear. I've set up the breakfast buffet in the dining room. Help yourself."

Lauren debated skipping breakfast. She

wanted to be gone before Gage came downstairs, but her loudly rumbling stomach vetoed that idea. "Thanks."

"I'll be in the kitchen if you need anything."

Lauren nodded and headed for the ornately decorated burgundy dining room. Yesterday morning after Gage had headed for the job site, Esmé and Leon had given Lauren a guided tour and history of the house. Her hosts' passion for their restoration project showed the hard work had been a true labor of love.

It wasn't until after Lauren had left for the Internet café that she'd realized the couple had pried more personal details out of her than she'd ever shared with anyone else, and Lauren hadn't even seen it coming. But that was okay. Her hosts were harmless. They would never use what they'd learned against her. Unlike Gage, who probably used every tidbit of information as a weapon in his arsenal.

Lauren shook her head as she cut through the doily-and-lace-accented living room. Surprisingly, she liked the house. The decor was frilly and feminine and a bit over the top—a huge contrast to the unadorned home she'd shared with her father. There'd been no time, interest or money for superfluities. The Lynch household had been all about practicality and purpose.

Her father's no-nonsense nature was one of the reasons she knew he wouldn't have purposely killed himself...unless he'd truly believed the life insurance money would have paid off Falcon Air's debts.

Oh, Dad, why did you borrow so much against the company?

Suppressing the stab of grief, she grabbed a plate from the sideboard. Worrying and second-guessing wouldn't solve anything, and even if she could eventually get her mother to sit still long enough to fill in the blanks, the FAA's investigation would likely determine whether or not her father's life insurance paid out. If it didn't...

She didn't want to think about that, didn't want to think about losing Falcon Air or what she and Lou would do without the company that had been everything to them. Lou hadn't worked anywhere else since before Lauren had been born, and he was a bit set in his ways. Starting over at sixty would be difficult for him *if* he could find a job.

Her stomach twisted, whether from hunger or nerves or both, she couldn't be sure. But she couldn't resist the delicious-smelling selection on the sideboard. Her mouth watered in anticipation of sampling the crisp bacon, maple sausage, vegetable-filled mini omelets and silver-dollar pancakes topped with cinnamon apples.

Grimacing at the obscene amount of food she'd piled on her plate, she carried it to the table. She'd just lifted her fork when Gage walked in wearing one of his perfectly fitting suits, this one in charcoal with a smoke-gray shirt and a black patterned tie.

He swept her with those dark eyes. "You'll have to change."

She didn't like the sound of that. "Why?"

"Because you're coming with me."

Definitely not what she wanted to hear. She'd only seen a tiny corner of San Francisco. "I thought we weren't flying out until Monday."

"We're going to the computer component plant I've come to assess. If you're studying business management, then you need to view the principles firsthand and see if you've learned enough to apply your book knowledge."

The idea both attracted and repelled her. She was eager to learn anything that might help her untangle Falcon Air's financial issues when she returned home. Yesterday while she'd been sitting in the coffee shop she'd done a little Web surfing research on her passenger. According to three major business magazines, Gage was reportedly one of the best corporate troubleshooters in the country.

Maybe he could help her with Falcon?

No. He was looking for something to discredit her, and he was her brother's spy. Trent didn't need the kind of ammo Falcon's iffy finances would provide to use against her.

The chemistry between her and Gage was an additional complication, especially now that she'd seen him half-naked. Wasn't it bad enough that she relived that kiss every time she closed her eyes? Now she'd see him shirtless, too. She'd bet a tank of fuel that reel would replay in her head.

Spending the day with him was too risky.

"That's an interesting idea, Gage, but I have other plans."

"You'll go." His flat, don't-argue-with-me tone raised her hackles and stirred her temper.

She looked at the breakfast she no longer wanted then at the man she wanted nothing to do with. Was this one of those commands Trent had insisted she comply with? "I take it no isn't an option?"

"Correct." Gage crossed to the buffet. While he filled his plate she debated calling her half brother and screaming at him. It wouldn't accomplish anything. She knew Trent would take sides—and it wouldn't be hers. But venting would make her feel better. Unfortunately, dramatic hissy fits had never been her style.

But damn her half brother for putting her in this position. Shadowing clients was not in her job description. In fact, under normal circumstances, she would have dumped her passenger in San Francisco, gone back on the assignment roster and returned to pick Gage up three days later. HAMC pilots did not sit around and twiddle their thumbs while their clients worked multiday deals. The flight crews filled the hours of their five-days-on-five-days-off schedules flying other customers.

"And if I don't want to go with you?"

"Why would you pass on the chance to see your textbook theories put into practice unless you're not really interested in learning?"

Something about his tone rubbed her the wrong way. "What are you insinuating?"

"That perhaps you're playing at being a student until a better opportunity comes along."

"What kind of opportunity?"

"A rich mother. A guaranteed job. A wealthy lover."

She gasped. Anger boiled in her veins. "I see my half brother has been digging."

Gage's eyes narrowed. "You have a lover waiting in the wings?"

Okay, maybe Trent hadn't been snooping through her past and uncovered Whit. Just as well. She didn't want to explain how stupid she'd been to believe Whit would marry a nobody like her simply because they'd been long-term lovers. He'd dumped her as soon as the right kind of woman came along.

"My personal life is none of your business unless it affects my ability to keep you safe in the air." She shot to her feet, fists curled by her sides, determined to get as far away from Gage as possible.

"Your accusations are unfounded. I'm a damned good pilot and better qualified than half of HAMC's roster. Ask your buddy Trent. He'll verify that, although he'll probably choke on the words.

"As for not wanting to learn… You're way off base, Faulkner. My father is dead. Falcon Air is now half-mine. I want to learn everything I can about running it, but I don't see how trailing after you will benefit me."

"Because I'm the best at what I do."

A snort burst from her. "Lack of confidence clearly isn't an issue for you."

"Nor you."

She gritted her teeth on the desire to tell him to go to hell. "It's Saturday."

"There are fewer interruptions from employees on weekends. The CEO and a skeleton staff will be on board to provide what we need." He sat across from her and dug into his food. His appetite clearly hadn't been killed by the idea of spending a day with her.

The door to the kitchen swung open and Esmé breezed in with a coffee carafe before Lauren could make her escape. Esmé looked at Lauren's plate. "Oh, good, dear. I'm so glad you have an appetite. I love to cook, and it pains me when the fruits of my labor go to waste. So many of your contemporaries practically starve themselves with that no-fat-no-carbohydrates garbage."

Feeling trapped, Lauren eyed the mountain of food on her plate and resigned herself to forcing it down rather than disappointing her hostess even though she knew the man across from her was going to give her indigestion. A full day of it.

Lauren stared at the pile of purchasing orders Gage had given her and fought the urge to roll her eyes.

Busywork. Nothing your average twelve-year-old couldn't do. She certainly didn't need a business degree to handle what was essentially categorizing and organizing the computer plant's purchasing history. But she wouldn't complain. He probably wanted to make her miserable. The jerk. And that was one payoff she refused to give him.

At the other end of the long boardroom table in the windowless room Gage looked engrossed in something interesting. Fighting the urge to wad up a piece of paper and hurl it at him like a snowball, she swiveled her chair sideways so she wouldn't have to look at him and crossed her legs. Her foot kicked in irritation. She should be out seeing the sights.

Her best bet was to get through this garbage

and make him find something else for her to do—preferably something that required brain cells.

She sorted, stacked and tabulated, adding comments on a pad of paper as she worked until she'd finished the pile. Relieved, she shoved it aside and checked her watch. Two hours. Wasted.

"Done."

He hit her with another one of those intense looks, the kind he'd been shooting at her while she worked, the ones she'd been trying to ignore, then he frowned and scanned the neatly paper-clipped piles on her desk. "You're finished?"

"Yes. What else do you have for me?"

He lay down his pen, rose and headed in her direction. "Let me see."

She stood and walked away from the table to stretch the kinks from her spine rather than be near him. The staff had left refreshments for them. She selected a diet soda loaded with caffeine from a mini fridge and popped it open. The cool liquid slid down her throat, reviving her somewhat.

She didn't mind paperwork, not really, but she'd rather be behind the controls of a plane than behind a desk. Her father had been the same way. That's why they'd needed Uncle Lou—who was a whiz with numbers.

"You made these notes?"

Gage's question made her turn. He held the yellow legal pad she'd written on. "Yes."

He flipped through the pages. "You've made a good point. By not forming a continuous relationship with one supplier our client is paying a wide range of prices for the same products and not benefiting from customer loyalty discounts."

"*Your* client," she corrected. "Every business has its own version of the frequent flyer rewards plan." Falcon always ordered their parts and fuel from the same suppliers.

"I'll get you something else to work on." He crossed to a file cabinet and extracted another manila folder. "You'll find this a little more challenging."

She flipped through the pages. "The company has an investment portfolio?"

"See which ones you think they should keep and which they should unload." He returned to his end of the table.

"Gage, if they need liquid cash, why do they have these investments at all? It's not like the company needs a retirement account. That's more of a personal thing. Besides, none of these brings in big dividends. In fact, some have lost quite heavily."

He met her gaze again this time with respect and admiration in his dark eyes instead of dislike and distrust. "Good observation. When you've finished that, I'll give you the notes I've made on the project thus far, including a transcript of my initial interview with the CEO. Read over them while I finish up for today, then give me two lists. First, the additional data you'd like to see, and second, options you think the company should consider."

Surprise made her eyebrows shoot up. That sounded almost like…teamwork. Was it another test? Or did he actually want to hear what she had to say? She couldn't help but be suspicious. "You want my opinion. Why?"

"You offer a fresh perspective."

"Right. Like that compares to a trained professional."

"Lauren, you think outside the box. You're not constrained by knowledge of what has worked or not worked in similar situations in the past the way a seasoned consultant might be."

That sounded like a compliment.

"Okay." She'd give him her opinion and then maybe she could still get some sightseeing done.

But if he kept looking at her that way, as if he might actually enjoy having her here, then there was going to be trouble, because she didn't want him to like her.

And she absolutely did not want the feeling to be mutual.

He'd underestimated his opponent, Gage admitted as he shoved open the beveled-glass front door of the B and B Saturday evening. "Show me your paper."

Lauren turned on her low heels. "My economics paper? Why?"

She'd worn her black HAMC uniform skirt and a plain white blouse today. The conservative outfit should have made her look prim and stiff, but at some point during the day she'd twisted her hair up on the back of her head and stuck a pencil in it to hold it in place, resulting in a spiky spray. She looked young and fresh and smart. A sexy brainiac.

Gage rejected the idea, but he couldn't get rid of the reluctant respect she'd earned from him today. He'd expected her to be deadweight and a real pain in the ass. He had a packed schedule and no time or interest in babysitting, but he'd had no choice except to drag her along if he wanted to keep her from contacting her mother.

He'd given Lauren busywork to keep her out of his way. She'd dug right in without complaint and come up with several interesting and intelligent observations. She'd ended up saving him time and giving him a perspective he wouldn't have considered otherwise. They'd actually worked well together, but their truce was an uneasy one.

Esmé entered the foyer carrying two glasses. "You're just in time. It's south of the border night. Have a mojito while I put the finishing touches on dinner."

She pressed tall glasses of iced clear liquid into Gage's and Lauren's hands. Green leaves and slices of lime floated near the bottom and white crystals clung to the rim.

"I'll see you two in the dining room. Dinner's in twenty minutes." She headed back to the kitchen, her loose dress floating behind her like curtains blown by a breeze through an open window.

He focused on Lauren who eyed her glass and then him. "I'm not flying you anywhere until Monday, right?"

"Yes."

"Good. Then I can have this. I love mojitos." She pursed her lips and sipped. Her eyes closed and her lips curved upward. "Mmm. Mmm. Minty and sweet."

A crystal clung to her lip. A pass of her tongue wiped it away. He pried his gaze from her mouth and focused on the cold glass sweating in his hand. The sound she'd made had been close enough to a moan to sound almost sexual. An unwanted image of her face flushed, not in the anger he'd deliberately aroused this morning, but in desire filled his brain.

He blinked to clear his head. "I want to see the paper you e-mailed to your teacher."

She took another sip, watching him with a skeptical gaze from beneath her lashes. "Why? You think I lied about it?"

He'd earned her antagonism. "Not after today. You had a keen grasp on the subject. I'm curious to see how far along you are in your studies."

"I have fifteen hours of classes left before I get my degree. I can't go full-time because of work and...well, money."

Another reminder of what she stood to gain from her association with Jacqueline Hightower. But Lauren had shown she was a stickler for following rules. Would a rule follower stoop to shortcuts and swindling?

"I want to see it," he repeated.

Lauren stared at him then sighed and shrugged. "Sure. Why not? Maybe after you read it you can tell my half brother I'm not as stupid as he thinks I am."

"Trent has never called you stupid. And for what it's worth, I don't relay everything to him. What's between you and me is our business unless it directly concerns him."

Gage carefully filtered out the need-to-know facts. Thus far, there had been very few worth sharing. Trent had enough on his plate, and Gage always carried out his end of a bargain.

"You're deluded. The Hightower siblings are convinced I'm a greedy lying witch out to cast a spell on their mother and steal their inheritance."

He didn't bother to deny her dead-on assessment.

"What they don't bother to see is that if I'd really wanted to worm my way into Jacqui's affections or her wallet, I would have moved into the Hightower castle when she invited me. I wouldn't have found my own place."

He filed the info away. "Why didn't you?"

"Because I can't stand the idea of servants hovering around waiting to cook for me or clean up after me as if I was a child. Besides, I like my space and my independence." She pivoted and climbed the stairs.

Following her three treads behind, he tried not to focus on her rear end at his eye level. Tried and failed. Lauren was slender, but curved in all the right places. And she had great legs. Long legs. Whenever she'd been lost in thought today she'd crossed those sexy limbs at the knee and kicked her ankle, garnering far too much of his attention. She'd been a distraction. A delicious, delectable distraction.

He huffed out a breath. What in the hell was wrong with him? Acting on the growing attraction between them would bring nothing but trouble. For all he knew she could have been playing him with every shift of her tight little body.

But he didn't think so. He'd had women in hot pursuit since before he made his first million, and Lauren didn't give off those predatory signals. In fact, more often than not she acted as if she wished he weren't around—a novel, but not pleasant sensation.

Trent's theory was beginning to look shaky. Gage made a mental note to call his buddy to check the status on the missing money. Jacqueline could have simply gone shopping. It wasn't as if she hadn't dropped bundles of money on a whim before.

He knocked back a swig of his drink. Sweet, cold and refreshing after a long day. A little heavy on the rum. Not his usual Knob Creek bourbon, but not bad. He licked a grain of sugar from his lip. The action reminded him of Lauren doing the same downstairs. His body reacted with a physical kick he couldn't prevent.

He yanked his thoughts back to the woman in front of him. "This morning you said Trent had been snooping when I mentioned a rich lover."

Lauren shot a startled look at him over her shoulder as she stopped at her bedroom door. "Excuse me?"

"Do you have a lover waiting for you?" What

kind of man would let a woman like her out of sight for months on end?

"I'm not seeing anyone and haven't for…a while." She grimaced as if she regretted replying, unlocked her door and after an awkward hesitation stepped inside. "I don't have a printed copy of my paper. You'll have to read it on my laptop unless you have a portable printer."

"Not this trip." He set his briefcase on the floor by the door and scanned the room. Flowers and ruffles dominated the decor. Not surprising since most of the house looked as if it had been hit by a lace factory explosion. "Boot up."

She shifted on her feet and nibbled her bottom lip, clearly uncomfortable with him in her room. Then she squared her shoulders, crossed the Aubusson rug and sat at the rolltop desk. She opened her laptop and turned it on. Her room, like his, lacked a spare chair. He'd requested suites with bathrooms attached, but he'd booked at the last minute and both of those had already been taken by honeymoon couples he had yet to see, although he had heard some telltale knocking on the wall last night—presumably a headboard. When his assistant played back his dictation he'd probably wonder what in the hell Gage had been doing.

"What exactly were you looking for at the plant today?"

Lauren's question drew him back to the present. He sat on the edge of the pillow-laden bed within a yard of her and tried to engage his brain. Work was rarely a top priority when he visited a woman's bedroom. "Ways to increase efficiency and profitability. Cutting waste is usually the first step."

"Did you find some? You certainly took a lot of notes."

"I'm still assimilating data."

"Ah, yes. Assess, assimilate, communicate and implement," she quoted his earlier words back at him.

"You paid attention during the car ride to the location."

"Yep." Her unexpected smile punched the air

from his lungs. "Flying is all about acronyms. All I had to do was make up one to fit your strategy. AACI. Piece of cake. So now what?"

"I'll take the data I gather back to my office, and my team and I will go over it and brainstorm strategies for improvement."

"I would have expected you to fly solo."

She'd read him correctly. "Having a team of specialists allows us to take on more clients."

More clients meant more revenue. More revenue meant more investments. More investments meant a greater chance of financial security if his business failed. Watching his father's financial and mental collapse had taught Gage to always have Plans A, B and C ready to implement at a moment's notice.

Lauren swiveled in her chair to open the file on her computer, revealing the back of her neck and a tiny horseshoe-shaped birthmark just beneath her hairline. Trent had the same one. Gage had noticed it back in college when his buddy had sported a military buzz cut.

Gage couldn't take his eyes off Lauren's vulnerable nape. He tugged the pencil from her hair, letting the strands fall and cover temptation. The urge to test the texture of her hair was an unwelcome one.

Her spine went rigid and then relaxed. "Oops. Forgot about that. I stole a pencil. Internal theft—the curse of the corporate world."

The mischief in her eyes as she looked at him over her shoulder thickened his throat. "Return it tomorrow."

She lifted her glass, sipped and swallowed, once again drawing his eyes to her mouth the way a Dumpster draws flies.

"Tomorrow is Sunday."

"Still a workday."

"Don't take this the wrong way, Gage. Today was very interesting and informative. But I haven't been to San Francisco before, and I'd rather see more of it than the inside of a computer parts plant. My daddy always said take a little piece of everywhere you go home with you even if it's only in your heart, and I aim to do that."

If he turned her loose, she'd go back to that damned Internet café. "We'll work in the morning then sightsee in the afternoon and have dinner at Fisherman's Wharf tomorrow night. That means we'll have to work Monday morning, as well, and leave after lunch."

"We?" Equal parts wariness and excitement warred in her teal eyes.

"I've been here a few times. I'll show you around. But in return, you come to the plant and work with me."

Silence stretched between them. Her ankle kicked. "Another command appearance?"

"This is more of a personal request. I appreciated your assistance today."

"I guess that would be all right." She swiveled back to the computer. "Here's the document. I'll get out of your way."

She made to stand. He put a hand on her shoulder, holding her in her seat. The firmness of her muscles surprised him. It shouldn't have, not with the way she easily controlled her seven-hundred-pound motorcycle or an airplane that weighed several tons. "Don't move. I'll read over your shoulder. That way if I have questions you can see to what I'm referring."

"O…kay."

Gage set his drink on the desk, braced one hand on the polished surface and the other on the back of her chair and leaned forward. Her scent wafted up to him, floral, but faint enough he suspected it might be her shampoo rather than perfume. It took several moments for him to be able to focus on the words on the screen. As soon as he did she hooked him with her unique premise.

He reached past her to hit the key to turn the page, his forearm brushing hers. Heat scattered through him, but he disregarded it. Or tried to. Ten pages later, he nodded as he read the closing line.

An even deeper appreciation for her intelligence filled him as he turned his head to meet her gaze. "You've argued your theory quite well. Did you come up with the idea or did your professor assign a topic?"

"It's my idea. I like coffee, and I tend to buy a cup whenever I'm out running my weekly errands. I never have to drive more than a half mile out of my way to get it. But a lot of coffee shops don't stay in business long.

"In the rush to have a store convenient to every consumer, most franchises allow branches to open up too close together, thereby sabotaging their revenue base and dooming themselves to fail. Even some grocery stores have coffee shops now. The same applies to restaurants and retail chains. The businesses are their own worst enemy."

She bit her bottom lip as if expecting him to contradict her. But he couldn't. She was right. Too much of a good thing was never a good thing. But seeing doubt instead of her usual cocky confidence revealed a vulnerable side she'd been careful to hide from him up to this point.

Could this woman be the conniving bitch Trent claimed? She seemed too smart, too capable and too willing to work hard. Sure, Trent had been right about Angela, but Gage had become a decent judge of character since his ex-wife's stormy, expensive departure a decade ago. None of the women he'd allowed into his life since his divorce had fooled him.

Lauren dampened her lips again, drawing his attention to her mouth. The memory of the kiss they'd shared ambushed him with sensation and need. She must have read the hunger on his face because she gasped and her eyes widened.

"You're quite an impressive woman, Lauren Lynch. If you weren't such a damned good pilot, you'd make a good business consultant."

"Gage—"

He ignored her warning tone, leaned in and stole his name from her lips. She went rigid. But she didn't pull away. After a moment her mouth relaxed beneath his, and she sipped from him as he did from her. When he stroked her bottom lip with his tongue, she met him halfway. He tasted the sugar and mint of her mojito, but mostly he tasted Lauren. And he wanted more.

Desire raced through him like fire through an abandoned warehouse. He grasped her arms and lifted her from her seat, pulling her forward until her soft breasts rested against his chest and her thighs aligned with his.

Lauren's arms circled his waist, and her short nails scraped a path parallel to his spine, driving a spike of hunger through him. She kissed the way she rode a motorcycle, the way she flew a plane—with one hundred percent commitment. He stroked her hair, then tangled his fingers in the fine, silky strands to cradle her head while he deepened the kiss.

Her mouth was hot and wet and slick, and he couldn't get enough of her, couldn't hold her close enough. The mattress bumped the back of his legs. He wanted her on it. Flat on her back. Beneath him. Naked.

He swung her sideways until they both stood beside the bed. His hands shook as if he had a case of the D.T.'s when he reached for the buttons of her blouse. He freed the first, the second. Her hands covered his and she lifted her head with her eyes tightly closed, then her lids lifted, and she stared at him through her thick lashes. Her chest rose and fell beneath his knuckles, and the sound of their labored breathing filled the room.

Passion darkened her eyes and trembled on her lips, then with one blink uncertainty gave way to purpose. She caught his hands, opened his fingers and spread them over her breasts. The mounds filled his palms, beaded tips raking his flesh as he caressed her. She gasped. Her bra and blouse were in the way. He wanted skin.

Hunger so strong it hurt fisted in his gut. Struggling to regain control, he buried his mouth in her neck and inhaled her fragrance as he thumbed her nipples. He tasted the soft skin behind her ear. Her whimper filled the air.

She felt good and fit perfectly in his arms. He took her mouth again, diving deep with his tongue the way he wanted to drive his body into hers. Lauren responded by pressing her hips hard against his erection. He pushed back and heat detonated in his groin.

A bell tinkled in the distance. He ignored it, spread open Lauren's blouse and cupped the satiny triangles of her bra. His thumbs dipped into the cups, brushing over her tight nipples. She shivered and gave a little frustrated squeak that nearly buckled his knees then she broke the kiss.

"Dinner," she whispered against his mouth, her lips brushing over his with the word.

"Screw dinner."

A shocked laugh burst from her. Shaking her head she disentangled slowly, dragging her nails around his waist and across his abdomen which contracted involuntarily. A naughty grin curved her swollen mouth. "Tell that to Esmé and you'll break her heart."

Lauren's blouse, still tucked into her waistband, gaped open, revealing pale curves above the shiny fabric of her bra. Frustration clawed at him. He stepped toward her, but she retreated and held up both hands. "Don't."

"Lauren—"

"We can't do this, Gage. Not unless you can promise me it won't get back to Trent and cost me my job."

Trent. Duty. Debt. The sobering realization that

he'd forgotten all three. At the moment he didn't give a damn. "You want me as much as I want you."

She inhaled deeply and exhaled slowly. Her hand lifted as if to touch his face, but she quickly withdrew it and tucked it behind her back. "Yes, I want you. But that doesn't mean I can afford to follow through."

Six

What were you thinking?

Lauren mentally kicked her own behind as she hurried toward the dining room, running from the mistake she'd almost made. She might be adventurous professionally, but she'd always been cautious in her personal life, her sex life in particular. How had Gage made her forget that?

Surprise stopped her in the dining room entrance when she spotted two other couples already seated at the round table. Gage bumped into her, searing his full body length against her back for one brief pulse-skipping moment. He grasped her waist to steady her, and her breasts and lips tingled, asking—no, *begging*—for more of what she'd sampled upstairs.

The man could kiss. Not even with Whit, the man she'd thought herself in love with and hoped to marry, had she ever felt anything as potent or exciting as the passion Gage had stirred in her.

Desire for Gage still gnawed at her, but that was one hunger she had every intention of denying. She shook off his hands and wished she could blame her loss of control on alcohol, but she'd consumed less than half of her mojito. The guilt rested squarely on her thirteen-months-and-counting celibate shoulders.

"Hi," she greeted the group and then stifled a wince at her overly loud, overly cheerful voice.

Esmé bustled in from the kitchen. "There you are. I was about to send Leon looking for you."

Lauren's cheeks burned like a hot lightbulb, and so did a certain spot below her navel. She hoped the others couldn't read on her face what she and Gage had been doing upstairs before coming down.

"Meet our other guests. Sue and Rob are from Utah." Esmé pointed first at the thirtysomething couple whose arms were entwined like mating snakes then at the fresh-faced couple who looked younger than Lauren. They seemed busy—under the table—if their overly innocent expressions and flushed cheeks were any indicator. "Tracy and Jack are from outside of Austin. Folks, meet Lauren and Gage."

Lauren would have guessed the couples were newlyweds even if Esmé hadn't told her about the B and B's other guests during the tour. The couples' devotion showed in every lingering glance and touch. It was as if the partners couldn't bear to be physically disconnected even though they sat only inches apart.

The only chairs left at the table were side by side. Gage pulled one out for Lauren then took the other spot. Their arms and shoulders brushed as they unfolded cloth napkins, making Lauren's already-agitated synapses crackle like a lightning storm. Another leaf in the table would have given them more room.

The couple across from her kissed, rubbed noses and shared an intimate smile. Their lovey-dovey, touchy-feely antics drove home to Lauren what she could be doing right now if she didn't care about her job, and if she could ignore the fact that she'd disliked the man beside her until sometime today.

She tried to remember at what point she'd realized she no longer hated Gage. It wasn't on the drive to the plant this morning when he'd informed her in a superior tone how he operated and what he expected of her. The change might have started when she'd looked up to find him watching her from across the paper-strewn boardroom table with respect and admiration in his dark eyes instead of dislike and distrust. Or maybe the antagonism had faded when he'd offered her a more challenging task than the busywork he'd initially assigned her, or when he'd started working with her as a partner instead of an opponent.

Esmé served another round of mojitos before Lauren could refuse. Inhibition-lowering alcohol was the last thing she needed when her will-power was already shaky. Leon came in carrying a large tray. He unloaded platters of chiles rellenos, Spanish rice and frijoles charros in the center of the long table. The heady aroma of the stuffed peppers and spicy beans with sausage made Lauren's mouth water. Mexican cuisine had always been her favorite. Esmé added bowls of guacamole, pica de gallo, sour cream and finely shredded lettuce.

"Serve yourselves family style," Esmé said before returning to the kitchen.

Lauren reached for the closest platter. Gage did the same simultaneously.

"Allow me," he said as he grasped the spoon.

Lauren jerked her hands away and stuffed her fists in her lap. Another round of sparks bounced from her knuckles to her nipples at the near miss.

She fastened her gaze on his hands. Those long fingers had caressed her breasts—breasts currently tingling with a plea for round two. His short clipped nails had grazed her with devastating effectiveness. She hoped he didn't notice the tenting of her blouse when he put a serving of the chiles on her plate.

After spooning his own, he twisted to pass the platter to the newlywed beside him. His thigh nudged hers beneath the table. She moved her leg away, but too late. Heat rushed to the point of contact.

She accepted a bowl of rice from the woman to her right, took a serving then offered the dish to Gage. Their gazes met over the bowl. His fingers covered hers. The promise of passion darkened his eyes to the color of rich cocoa as he took the dish from her. Heat swirled in her belly leaving her feeling a lot like a melting marshmallow. She almost dropped the rice.

He repeated his actions as the remainder of the food circled the table, and each time his thigh and fingers lingered longer against hers. Lauren's appetite for food diminished, while her appetite for the man beside her filled her with an empty ache.

She shot him a narrow-eyed look. Was he deliberately tormenting her? Teasing her? Arousing her?

She'd bet her bike on it. Gage wasn't the kind of man to do anything accidentally. She'd bet each touch above and below the table was calculated for seduction.

Maybe she ought to give in. Go for it. Take the pleasure he offered for however long it lasted. Trent was going to find a reason to fire her sooner or later anyway, and she was beginning to believe she would never get any more out of her mother, who hadn't returned any of Lauren's calls since their chat the other night and had even left the country to avoid a face-to-face chat.

Mayday, Mayday, Mayday, her brain shrieked. *Don't be an idiot.*

One side of Gage's eyebrows lifted in a silent taunt as if he could hear her internal argument.

Oh, man, he should know better than to dare her like that. For pity's sake, hadn't he figured out by now that she thrived on challenges? She hadn't garnered all her certifications by backing down when the hotshot flyboys tried to push her around. She'd learned to fight back. There was no better way to shut up a cocky SOB than to best him. It would serve Gage right if she—

An idea struck her and a wicked chuckle danced in her chest, but she suppressed it. She had less luck curbing the smile taking control of her mouth. He wanted a fight, did he? She could certainly give him one. She could play footsie and tease as well as he could. Let's see how he responded to being bested at his own game.

Beneath the table, she shed her shoe and found his ankle with her toes. His start of surprise repaid her for every irritating jab he'd taken at her expense. Without glancing her way, he shifted his foot out of reach and lifted his fork as if nothing out of the ordinary had occurred.

Disappointed, Lauren mirrored his actions and blindly searched for her shoe. Before she could find it, his foot—now clad only in a sock—covered hers, pinning it to the hardwood floor. Her body went rigid. She almost shoved her fork up her nose and only at the last minute found the target of her mouth.

His heat seeped into her skin and crept up her leg, heading directly toward a recently awakened area. She gently tugged to no avail. He had her trapped. She couldn't escape without an undignified struggle, and she wouldn't give him that satisfaction.

She didn't look at him as she chewed without tasting and debated her next move. A few bites later she wiggled out of her other pump, crossed her leg and dragged the tip of her toe down his thigh. He coughed as if he'd choked on his rice and reached for the napkin in his lap. Only he didn't grab his napkin. He grabbed her foot and held it tightly to his hard thigh.

Her smile died. Lauren scanned the other guests, but the couples were too engaged in each other and dinner to notice the antics going on around them.

Gage caressed her instep with his thumb, firmly sweeping from her heel forward. Good thing she wasn't ticklish.

With his other hand he casually continued his meal. How could he chew and swallow when she could barely think or breathe? Determined not to let him know he'd rattled her, she picked up her fork and fed herself by rote. Conversation buzzed around her, but her mind focused on her captive foot and those caressing fingers. And payback. Oh, yes, there would definitely be payback for his shenanigans.

She tried to extricate herself without luck. He rubbed deep circles on the ball of her foot. She nearly moaned in pleasure. She'd never had a foot massage before. It could become addictive.

The man didn't fight fair.

But then, what man did?

And of course, his lack of fair play meant she could fight dirty, too. She dropped her hand beneath the table and curled her fingers around his wrist. His grip on her instep tightened, but she had no intention of prying him loose. Her goal was to disconcert him as much as he had her. She raked her nails lightly up the inside of his arm. He shivered almost imperceptively, which only encouraged her to repeat the action. Gage cut her a sideways look so blistering hot she almost melted in her chair like ice cream on a Daytona sidewalk in July.

He repaid her by dragging his thumbnail along the arch of her foot, and a ripple of desire washed over her. She never would have considered getting her foot scratched erotic, but boy, was she wrong. Her heart raced and her skin steamed.

Gage challenged her at every turn, making her mentally sharper and more focused and driven. She even kind of liked his confident swagger. Battling with him made her feel more alive than she had since her father's death.

Unless he'd been honest when he said he didn't tell Trent everything, taking their relationship to the next level could cost her her job. Did she dare trust him?

Her gaze fell to Gage's mouth—the one she wanted on her. On her lips. On her breasts. Everywhere.

A quiet breath whistled through his teeth, drawing her gaze back to his. He knew. She didn't know how he'd read her thoughts, but he knew she wanted him. And the sexual promise expanding his pupils and adding a tinge of red to his skin said the feeling was mutual.

He gave her foot a squeeze then stroked up her shin to her knee and down her calf to her ankle. His thumbnail scraped a deliciously light circle around her anklebone, but his gaze fell to her breast. Her nipples received the signal and hardened beneath her shirt. He flicked a finger-tip over the point of the tiny bone, but she felt it in her breasts, in her lap.

How could she possibly resist him? He was smart, gorgeous and ambitious—her big three.

Sleeping with Gage was one test flight she yearned to take. Admitting it sent a beehive buzzing through her. *If* she did this crazy thing, she wouldn't fool herself into believing any intimacy between them would lead to forever. They had too much against them. His wealth. His friendship with Trent. Her loyalty to Falcon Air. Living in different states.

She looked at her half-full plate. How long

before they could escape? She shoved a big bite into her mouth. The pepper, stuffed with creamy cheese and pork, was one of her favorite dishes, but it wasn't what she craved tonight.

"What about you, Lauren?"

The young newlywed's voice startled Lauren into swallowing in one big gulp. Her cheeks burned from an altogether different kind of heat than the rest of her body. "I'm sorry?"

"Where are you from?" the bubbly blonde asked.

"Daytona, Florida."

"Is your family still there?"

The loss struck again, like a cloud obscuring the sun. "No. My father died recently."

Gage released Lauren's foot. She put it back on the floor and shoved both feet into her shoes.

"What about your mom?"

The inevitable question. "I was raised by my father and his partner."

"Your daddy's gay?" Blondie sounded shocked. Her husband tried to shush her.

Lauren winced. "Sorry. I meant his business partner."

"No revolving door of girlfriends?"

"No. My father only loved one woman in his life, and since he couldn't be with her, he chose to be alone." Lauren felt Gage's eyes on her, but didn't turn.

"Why couldn't he? Did she die, too?"

"Tracy," her husband scolded in a whisper. "I apologize. We're from a small town where everybody knows your business."

Lauren waved away his concerns. "It's okay. My mother was and still is married to someone else. Trust me, I didn't miss what I didn't have."

That wasn't completely true. She'd had friends in school who didn't have fathers, but none who didn't have mothers. She'd often wondered why she had to be different. But her father had always said, "Your momma can't be with us, sugar," and that had been all Lauren could get out of him until that day she'd turned eighteen and been enlightened. Too little, too late.

As an adolescent she'd concocted a complicated story about her mother's tragic death in childbirth, but it turned out her girlish fantasies had been just that. The truth was her mother had chosen not to be with her except for a brief visit once each year. Jacqui had preferred her other children. That still stung.

"Are you two—" Sue, the other woman at the table pointed to Gage then Lauren "—together…like a couple?"

"No."

"No," Lauren replied hastily and simultaneously with Gage.

"What do you do, Lauren?" Sue persisted.

"I'm a pilot. Gage is a client of the company I work for." Beneath the table Gage gave her knee a squeeze, then a tormenting caress, shattering her concentration. "I fly airplanes and sometimes helicopters."

Brilliant, Lauren. What else would you fly? Kites?

She couldn't think with Gage drawing circles on her thigh with his fingertip. She shot him a warning glare. He winked and her stomach swooped.

She swallowed and turned back toward the other woman. "Gage is the one with the exciting job. A top business magazine voted him as the man you most want on your side in an economic downturn."

All eyes turned toward Gage. His caressing hand stilled, then withdrew. "I'm a business consultant."

"What does a business consultant do?" Tracy asked.

Two can fight dirty, Lauren decided. She slid her hand to Gage's thigh and lightly dug in her nails. His muscles went rock hard beneath her fingers.

"Consult. Owners. On. Improvement. Strategies." His carefully enunciated words made her lips twitch.

"AACI." She nudged him with her elbow, earning a narrow-eyed stare. Thanking heaven for the long tablecloth hiding her actions, she wiggled her fingers and batted her lashes like an innocent schoolgirl.

He covered her hand with his, flatting her palm against his leg. When she tried to pull free he laced his fingers through hers and anchored her.

"I assess the company's needs, assimilate the data, communicate my findings and help them implement a plan to reach their desired goals—usually financial goals, but some of my consultants specialize in other areas of industrial and corporate management."

"I got to see him in action earlier. He's very good." Lauren added the last tongue in cheek with a brief glance at his mouth.

Fire kindled in his eyes at her double entendre. He didn't look away as he continued, "Lauren is also very…skilled. She's impressed the hell out of me thus far. I can't wait to see what else she has up her sleeves. Her passion…toward any project is quite extraordinary."

He wasn't talking about flying. Adrenaline rushed through her veins, making her almost light-headed. "Just remember what I told you at our initial meeting. Mastering new…equipment is something of an obsession with me. I'll tackle anything you throw at me. In an airplane it's simply a matter of lift and thrust, and knowing how far you can push your machine before you…break it."

Gage's nostrils flared. Gold glinted in his irises. Challenge issued and accepted.

She had to be out of her mind to contemplate becoming intimate with him. But she couldn't seem to think about anything else. That kind of distraction in the cockpit could be disastrous.

The silence caught Lauren's attention. She broke the simmering connection with Gage and scanned the table to find each occupant plus Esmé and Leon staring at them. From the flushed cheeks and parted lips, she'd bet they'd guessed neither she nor Gage were talking about flying.

Esmé dusted her hands on her frilly apron. "I'll go finish the flan."

Rob, the newlywed who'd been silent until now, cleared his throat. "I… Esmé, I think we'll skip dessert. Right, angel?" He shot his wife a pleading look.

"Yes," Sue piped up. "Dinner was great. Thank you so much. But I think we need to…rest. We have a big day planned for tomorrow." They both rose and bolted from the room. Their giggles as they raced up the stairs echoed to the dining room. Nobody at the table could possibly doubt they were headed for something more active than sleep.

"Um, yes. Us, too," Tracy added with a smoldering look at her husband. "We have an early flight to catch."

Their departure left Gage and Lauren alone with their hosts. Leon shook his head. "Newlyweds. Always the same no matter where they're from. I can barely get them to the table, and when I do they don't stay long enough to finish a meal."

Lauren wished the floor would open up and swallow her. "I'm sorry. I really know how to kill a party, don't I? Folks usually don't run until I start talking about hydraulics or compression ratios."

Gage's expression turned wry. "Run men off often, do you?"

She grimaced. "Let's just say knowing more about a man's car than he does tends to shorten my list of potential suitors."

Leon chuckled as he gathered the other guests' empty plates. "That's all right, sweetie. If a man can be scared off, then you should let him go. Means he's not the one for you."

Esmé nodded. "I'll leave the coffee on the

counter and the flan in the fridge. You help your-selves to it whenever you're ready."

"Thank you, Esmé. Dinner was excellent," Gage replied.

The kitchen door swung shut behind Esmé and Leon. It was clear her hosts expected them to dash off to bed, too. Worse, part of Lauren wanted exactly that, even though she was sure it would be a big mistake. Tension invaded her muscles and her pulse quickened.

"You like playing with fire." Gage's deep, quiet voice rumbled over her.

"Apparently so do you."

He turned in his chair, his knee branding her thigh. "If we go upstairs now I'm going to strip you down, take you to bed and not let you out for flan or anything else before morning."

She gulped at the image he painted with his candor. Should she go against wisdom and take a risk? Or play it safe? Either way, she was pretty certain she'd be damned if she did and damned if she didn't.

Seven

Lauren's heart rose to her throat and pounded as heavily as it had the day she'd stood in the open door of an airplane at ten thousand feet, waiting to make her first solo skydiving jump.

Only the best pilots "flew by feel," trusting their instincts no matter what the gauges told them. She was one of those few, and her sixth sense had never let her down. That same gut feeling told her not to hold back now. But still, going to bed with a near stranger wasn't like her. This was risky business. But a risk she had to take.

Gage Faulkner. Her brother's spy. Her former enemy. And soon to be her lover.

Looking at him, she gathered her courage and took that final step past the point of no return. "I always thought flan was overrated."

Her words ignited a feral passion in Gage's eyes. A shiver of awareness raced over her, then he blinked and the untamed look vanished. Had she imagined his brief reaction?

He pushed back his chair, steadily, deliberately, and stood then grasped the wooden back of hers and helped her scoot away from the table. She rose on trembling legs.

His palm skimmed down her spine as light as air and settled at her waist. His heat seeped through her clothing, a steaming prelude to what she could expect if she didn't come to her senses in the next few moments.

No. Once she'd committed to a course she followed through. She wanted Gage, wanted to experience the powerful passion only he seemed to be able to summon from her. There was a reason why he'd come into her life now when she was grieving and confused. Her job was to figure out why. And she couldn't do that by running away from what he made her feel.

He guided her out of the dining room and up the stairs with firm pressure. They stopped outside her door. Her mouth dried and her toes curled inside her shoes. She inhaled deeply, but the light-headed, surreal feeling remained. Anticipation made her hands shake as she fished her key from her pocket and slipped it into the lock. She shoved open the door and stepped forward.

Gage grabbed her elbow, halting her on the threshold. "Be sure."

Those two simple words confirmed her decision. That he'd give her an opportunity to change her mind impressed her. Most guys who'd made it this far would push for more whether or not she had doubts. She only had one concern. "This is between you and me? No Trent?"

His unflinching, gold-flecked gaze held hers. "No Trent."

She dampened her dry lips. "Then come in and make love with me, Gage."

The hunger in his eyes entranced her. Unable to look away, she backed into her room and he followed, pausing only to lock the door behind him.

The high mattress bumped the back of her thighs. Pulse pounding, she waited for him to close the distance between them. When only inches separated them she lifted her arms and pushed his suit coat off his shoulders. She caught it as it fell and tossed it on her desk chair. Next, she tackled his tie, loosening the knot until she could pull the silk free and drop it on top of his jacket.

He let her undress him. But while he didn't assist her, she knew he was far from passive. Leashed energy radiated from him. His fists bunched and released by his sides, and his dark eyes watched her, promising passionate payback with every button she freed on his shirt.

She resisted the urge to touch him for as long as possible. She lasted only five buttons before she gave in to the craving to trace the open V of tanned skin with her fingertips from collarbone to sternum to collarbone. His skin was warm, supple, addictive. His scent grew stronger, headier.

His respiratory rate quickened, mirroring hers. She yanked his shirttail free and quickly undid the remaining buttons then spread her hands over his chest, absorbing the warmth of his body and the feel of his heart hammering beneath her palm. She pushed the fabric out of the way, and his shirt fluttered to the floor. Splaying her palms on his chest, she caressed those gorgeous pecs, then his muscled shoulders, biceps and forearms.

The tightening pucker of his tiny nipples fascinated her. She had to touch him, but the nubs teasing her palms didn't satisfy her. She needed to taste him on her tongue. She leaned forward and licked him. His fingers speared through her hair, holding her close, and a groan rumbled from his chest, vibrating against her lips. The vibration traveled down her spine to her core.

His grip tightened momentarily then shifted to cradle her jaw and lift her head. He covered her mouth and devoured her with a barely restrained clash of teeth, lips and tongue. His arms looped around her back, yanking her flush against him. But it still wasn't close enough. Lauren ached for more. Skin on skin. Legs entangled. His body filling the expanding void in hers.

She forced her hands between them and tackled his belt buckle. In a frantic clash of kisses, desperate gasps, fumbling rushing fingers and grazing knuckles she hurried to remove the remainder of his clothing. Her arms tangled with his as he worked on her garments. This I'll-die-if-I-don't-have-you-now urgency was totally new to her.

Her skirt slipped to the carpet. Blindly, she kicked it and her pumps aside. The hem of her blouse teased her bottom like the stroke of a fingertip. Her skin was so sensitive that every shift of her clothing seemed like a caress. She reached for the button at her collar, but Gage broke the kiss and brushed her hands aside. "Let me."

He worked the buttons with more dexterity than she'd shown on his. When he finished, she shrugged her shoulders. For a fleeting moment as her shirt fluttered to the floor, she wished she was one of those girls who liked sexy, daring lingerie. But she'd been born with a practical streak. Her bra and bikini panties were relatively new, but still machine-washable, plain white satin without lace.

If Gage found her lingerie lacking, she couldn't tell by the hungry way his eyes ate her up with first one blistering sweep from her neck to her toes then with a slower, lingering return exploration. Her nipples tightened under his scrutiny. She couldn't wait to have his hands on her. His mouth. The thought stole her breath.

She silently cursed the panty hose required by her uniform. As if he understood her frustration, Gage hooked his thumbs in the unsexy garment and peeled her nylons down her legs. She stepped out of them.

He removed his socks, shoes and pants, and stood before her with his erection straining the silky fabric of his navy boxers.

Eager to touch him she flexed her fingers, but instead, she took the safer option and reached for the hooks on her bra. Gage stepped forward and his chest slapped against hers. He caught her hands behind her back, stopping her short of her goal. The navel to nipple contact and his mild bondage sent a thrill shooting through her.

She undulated against him, trying to get free. "Gage, I want you."

His nostrils flared on a swift inhalation. The line of hair bisecting his belly erotically tickled her stomach. "And I you."

He bent his head. His lips landed beneath her jawbone and worked their way south in butterfly-light touchdowns, brief, shocking, exhilarating kisses down the cord of her neck and over her collarbone. She quit struggling, willing to take whatever route he wanted to pursue. His lips traveled down the slope of one breast and up the other. She arched her back, silently begging him to take her into his mouth, but he ignored her plea.

He transferred her wrists into one of his hands and snapped her bra open with the other, then dragged one finger forward beneath the elastic, teasing the sensitive underside of her breasts. Her insides tightened as he lifted the cups, freeing her left nipple with a rasp of fabric across her overly responsive skin, then her right. The pad of his thumb grazed each tip, making her gasp. Her eyes closed and her head fell back as pleasure constricted her muscles. A warm gust of breath was her only warning before his hot mouth covered her.

She moaned and tried to free her hands to no avail. She wanted to touch him. His teeth gently gripped a tight tip, warning her to be still and then his tongue flicked her captive flesh sending an even more intense shock of arousal through her.

When he lifted his head she wanted to scream in disappointment, but then he released her and quickly stripped her bra down her arms. Self-consciousness slithered through her as he stared at her, breathing through parted lips. She worked out and her body wasn't bad, but she wasn't lush centerfold material.

She reached for him, her fingers digging into his thick shoulders and pulling him closer. He skimmed his palms up from her waist and cupped her in his hands, his thumbs drawing circles over her aching breasts.

He bent to suckle her again, drawing deeply on one side while his fingers plucked and gently tweaked the other. Heat pooled low in her abdomen, and she squeezed her legs together, shifting restlessly as need pulsed within her with each draw of his mouth.

He straightened and shucked his boxers. Lauren's breath stalled in her chest. She hadn't been with many men, but none of them shared Gage's bragging rights.

Momentarily shaken over the magnitude of the step she was about to take, she turned her back on him to gather her composure while she ripped the covers down the bed. He wound his arms around her waist. His hot body blanketed her back, and his erection scorched the base of her spine seconds before his hands set her breasts ablaze.

His teeth and lips grazed her shoulder, the side of her neck, then tugged gently on her earlobe. He pushed her forward, bending her over the high mattress. The prostrate position startled her.

She wasn't used to letting herself be vulnerable. But before she could protest his short nails lightly scored her back, raking over her bottom and plowing a field of goose bumps in their wake.

He dragged her panties down her legs. After freeing them from her ankles, he made the return trip twice as slowly, pausing to tease the back of her thighs with his lips then trace and caress the curve of her bottom. By the time he reached her shoulders again he covered her like a stallion, but without entering her. He pulled away slowly, leaving another trail of kisses down her spine as his body heat eased off.

Confused by his retreat, she faced him in time to see him straightening from the pants he'd dropped on the floor with a condom in his hand.

Protection. She nearly groaned, but assured herself she would have remembered…eventually. She wasn't careless. Ever.

She had an unopened box in her flight bag. She'd bought it last year after she'd broken up with Whit, with the intention of going out and proving with a series of other men that Whit hadn't hurt her. But apparently anonymous sex just wasn't her thing. She hadn't been able to get past the fact that she had to like and respect a guy before sleeping with him. Until Gage, she hadn't been tempted by any other man since Whit dumped her.

She took the condom from him and placed it on the mattress. She'd waited a long time to make love again, and she wasn't going to rush it. First, she wanted to do a little exploring of her own. She lifted his hand and pulled one of Gage's fingers into her mouth, swirling her tongue around the tip. His muscles jerked tight, cording and revealing his perfect physique. He swallowed hard. She moved to the next finger and then the next until he grasped her hand and stopped her.

She curled the fingers of her other hand around his thick erection. His sharply indrawn breath rent the air. He covered her hand with his and stroked his length once, twice, showing her how he liked to be touched. Hot, satiny skin covered a rock-hard arousal, and caressing him triggered a burst of hunger in her belly. She swept over the slick droplet on his tip with her thumb.

"You do like to play with fire." His voice rumbled low and deep like an approaching Boeing 787. He released her, gripped her waist and lifted her onto the bed then positioned himself between her knees. The position put them eye to eye until he captured her hands, lifted them over her head and urged her back on the cool sheets with her legs hanging over the side.

The position left her open and vulnerable, a little uneasy and a lot turned on. He captured a nipple in his mouth and stroked downward from her fingertips to her hypersensitive armpits. His hands mapped her body while his tongue traced the terrain of one breast then the other. Gage's ultralight touch swept her waist, then her belly and thighs, showering her with goose bumps and shivers.

Urgent need coalesced into a tight ball at her bikini line. She wound her legs around his hips and pulled him closer, but he didn't fill her as she craved. He only rested his arousal against her, hot and hard and heavy.

His teasing fingertips dipped closer and closer to her center with each pass until she strained toward his hand. And then finally, finally, when she thought she'd die from frustration, his fingers slid into her curls. He found her slick opening and stroked her. The intense shock of pleasure made her body bow. She cried out. "That… feels…good."

He zeroed in on exactly the right spot, circling again and again, drawing her deeper and deeper into a vortex where nothing else in the world mattered but the way he sucked, nipped and licked her breasts and plied her body. Her legs shook with need as she had never felt before, then she was hurled through a wind tunnel of sensation that pulled her in too many different directions to process. All her neurons seemed to crackle and hiss then explode in a shower of sparks.

When the spasms stopped, she tried to catch her breath. Even before the tingles receded from her toes, Gage's lips blazed a path down her midline toward the place his talented fingers had just vacated. "Gage, you don't have to—"

"I have to know how you taste."

His rough growl rocked her to her core, but that was nothing compared to the first lash of his tongue. Air filled her lungs in a rush. Lauren closed her eyes as every thought and all of her energy zoomed into tight focus on the magic Gage created with his mouth, with his hands. He cupped her buttocks and lifted her to love her with his tongue. The brand of each pad of his fingers burned her skin.

It was too much. Too good. Too fast.

She dug her nails into the sheets and fought to hold off her climax, to stall the shockingly swift ascent. Her senses sharpened, sabotaging her. Gage's scent mingled with hers in her nostrils. She could smell her arousal and his musky aroma. Without effort or intention on her part each of her muscles drew taut. But the coup de grâce, the final straw that snapped her control was the rasp of his five o'clock shadow on her tender flesh as he buried his face between her thighs.

Orgasm snatched her up like the sudden breath-stealing jerk of a parachute opening. Her free fall stopped abruptly and wave after wave of pleasure buffeted her. The hammering of her heart sounded like wind whipping the canvas 'chute. She felt as if she floated, dangled, then touched down with a gentle bump as he laid her on the mattress.

Reality slowly returned. Left weak by the most violent orgasm of her life, she pried her heavy lids open as Gage ascended her body, entangling her in a series of kisses and caresses over her hip bones, her belly, her waist and breasts until his lips reached hers.

He stole the breath she'd barely caught with a ravenous kiss and then eased up to meet her gaze. "You taste delicious."

A fresh gust of arousal blew through her. How had he decimated her that way? Why him? But she had no time to ponder her question. He reached for the condom, tore the packet and rolled it on, then he scooped her up like a limp rag doll and moved her to the middle of the bed, laying her parallel to the pillows.

She snapped out of her lethargy and pulled him closer with her arms, with her legs. The touch of his body at her entrance made her stiffen in anticipation of his first thrust, and he didn't disappoint. With one long, slow glide he filled her deeply, completely.

"Mmm," she sighed against his neck and stroked the bunched muscles of his back.

His whistled inhalation filled her ear. "Damn, you feel good."

"So do you." The weight of him, scent of him, feel of him surrounded her, impaled her. He withdrew. She pulled him back. Impatiently. Eagerly. Hungrily. He set a rhythm and she matched it, digging her heels into the mattress and countering each thrust. She kissed and nipped the cords of his neck, earning an encouraging growl. In return he grazed her ear with his teeth, with his tongue, steamed her neck with his breath and then stole hers with his voracious kisses.

The muscle-quaking tension returned, increasing with each thrust, as another orgasm built within her. She curled her nails into his tight butt and urged him faster, faster. She was close, so close. And then she was there, free-falling, crying out, clinging to him. His pace quickened, deepened, then his own groan of release echoed off the walls.

Heavy heartbeats later Gage eased down on her, bracing the majority of weight on the tripod of his arms and hips. She wound her arms around his waist and savored the feel of his cheek and chest pressed against hers and his breath bellowing near her ear.

Why did Gage have to be the one to destroy her girlish illusions? She'd always believed the kind of magical connection they'd shared would only come with love and trust and commitment. But she barely knew him and she certainly wasn't in love with him. As for a future with him…well, it had never crossed her mind.

Evaporating sweat cooled her body and cleared her head, allowing doubts to edge in. What she had with Gage could never be more than temporary, and she hoped it wouldn't come back to haunt her.

She prayed she hadn't made a mistake in lying with the man who until today had been her enemy.

Gage knew he'd crossed the line by sleeping with his best friend's sister—*half* sister. His personal ethics made his friend's relatives and exes off limits. But he'd broken that rule with Lauren. He hadn't been able to stop himself.

He levered himself off her and lay on his back by her side with his chest still heaving. Their knuckles touched on the mattress, and he had the strange urge to wrap his fingers around hers and hold her hand. Weird. *Damned* weird. He resisted the urge. He wasn't the hand-holding type.

Staring at the ceiling, he tried to work up a twinge of regret for his actions but failed. Maybe once his chest didn't feel as though it was going to explode and his legs had regained a little strength, he'd find a little remorse.

Lauren lay beside him with her eyes closed, but he could tell she wasn't asleep by her carefully modulated breathing and the tension radiating from her.

Her thick lashes slowly lifted and she turned her head. The satisfied expression in her eyes jumpstarted his slowing heart rate. "That was…"

"Amazing." He finished her breathless sentence when she didn't. He couldn't remember ever having sex that satisfying or intense before.

A smile twitched her swollen lips. She quickly captured it between her teeth. "Yes, it was. But, Gage, I'm not sure it was a good idea."

His thoughts exactly.

Her eyebrows dipped. "Maybe we should forget this ever happened."

What? He wasn't used to women wishing they hadn't slept with him. And he didn't like it. "I dare you."

"I beg your pardon?"

He rolled on his side, his weakened muscles protesting the call to action. She mirrored his move, displaying the curve of her hips and deep

V of her waist. One long, slender leg bent, hiding the triangle of dark blond curls from him. But he didn't need to see her. He remembered how she looked, smelled, tasted.

Regardless, he let his gaze travel slowly down her pale body. For a Florida girl she didn't have much of a tan, but she had a nice shape. Slender, curved, delicious. He swept a hand from her shoulder, down her arm and across her waist, settling on her hip. Her shiver brought the blood rushing back to his groin.

"I dare you to try to forget what we just shared." Rekindled arousal thickened his voice.

Her cheeks pinked and her pupils dilated. "Gage, it's not going to be easy to hide an intimate relationship from Trent. He's an ass, but he's not stupid. And I can't afford to get fired."

Damn. He'd never lied to Trent before. He didn't plan to start lying now. "How much longer will you work for HAMC? You said this was a temporary gig."

He wasn't thinking long-term relationship, but he wasn't ready to let her go until he worked whatever it was she'd done to him out of his system.

She reached behind her to snag a corner of the sheet and drag it over her hip. Gripping the pink fabric between her breasts, she glanced away. "I don't know. I don't want to leave until I—"

"Until you…what?"

"My mother has something I need."

That brought them back to the original reason Trent had called him. Regret climbed into the bed between them. Trent was convinced Lauren was a shyster. What if he was right?

"Money?" Gage spat out the word.

She flinched and met his gaze. "I've told you before I don't want the Hightowers' money. If you won't believe that especially after this, I'll quit wasting my breath."

Her lack of hesitation and the sincerity in her eyes convinced him she was telling the truth. But he'd been wrong before, and it had nearly cost him his home and his company. What if, once again, he'd let his dick do the thinking and been taken in by a beautiful woman?

No. Not this time. Everything he'd learned about Lauren contradicted Trent's summation of her personality.

"I believe you."

If nothing else came of their affair, Gage intended to prove Lauren's innocence to Trent even if that meant spending every possible moment with her and digging for the facts.

Eight

Lauren stared at Gage across the tiny window-side table at the Fisherman's Wharf restaurant. She'd never been more physically in tune with anyone before. But Gage was rich. He was Trent's friend. He lived in Knoxville.

Three strikes.

Four if you counted the fact that she'd only known him a week.

So why did she still want him when there was absolutely no way they could ever make this work?

Girl, you have it bad.

It's just a crush. No big deal.

She hoped.

After an afternoon of playing tourist, riding cable cars and walking the wharf, he was smiling, windblown, a little sunburned and completely relaxed—the opposite of the way he'd been the day she'd met him.

And she was completely smitten.

He looked up from the dessert menu and caught her staring. "I've been to San Francisco a dozen times and eaten on the Wharf half of those, but always at restaurants chosen by my clients. I've probably walked right by this place a few times."

"It's easy to miss crammed between two flashy tourist traps."

One corner of his mouth lifted. "I never would have considered polling the locals to ask who served the best seafood."

She swept a glance over the simple decor of the dining room. The plain wooden furniture and scarred hardwood floors weren't much to look at, but the view of the docks was incredible, and the food had been the best she'd had in ages. This was the kind of place she, her father and uncle adored. Her mother would have been horrified to eat here, as evidenced by the stilted restaurants Lauren had been forced to endure whenever her mother had visited in the past.

She pushed aside the unpleasant memories. "It's a habit I picked up when landing at unfamiliar airports. Locals know where to eat, and mom-and-pop cooks are usually more concerned with flavor than whether the food looks like artwork on the plate."

"After this—" he gestured to his empty plate "—I believe you." As he had after the motorcycle ride, he looked surprised that he'd enjoyed the day. What could make a man afraid to unwind?

They had barely been apart since they'd made love the first time last night. This morning they'd worked together before heading out to see the sights. But despite that, she barely knew him. Most of their conversation had centered around the attractions which he'd missed on previous visits.

"Gage, what do you do in your free time?"

"I don't have a lot of free time," he answered quickly.

"You can't work 24/7."

"I've been building Faulkner Consulting."

No wonder he looked older than his age. "My father had a couple of signs hanging in his office. The first said, 'Making a living is not the same as making a life.' And the second, 'Love what you do and do what you love.' He always claimed that if died—" A knot in her throat squeezed off her voice. She took a sip of her lemonade and tried again. "He claimed if he died living by those simple rules, then he would have had a full life. And he did."

Gage sat back in his chair, his face closing. "Idealism won't keep a roof over your head or food on the table. Sometimes chasing dreams isn't enough."

"I disagree. We should all be lucky enough to pursue our dreams." She had to believe that. Otherwise, her father's life and death were pointless.

Damn her mother. What possible purpose did

it serve for Jacqui to refuse to discuss that final conversation with Kirk? Lauren fisted her hands. Enough waiting already. As soon as she got home she was going to corner her mother and make her talk.

"I'd prefer not to have to worry about where my next meal is coming from."

"Like you did when you were a child?"

"Yes. But I prefer not to dwell on the past. It's over and can't be changed." He covered her hand on the table. "Let's get out of here."

The deep rumble of Gage's voice and the sensual promise flickering to life in his eyes quickened her heartbeat and sent heat coursing through her. There was absolutely no doubt in her mind that if they left now, they were going back to the B and B and straight to bed. If she chose to delay and question him further, she'd kill the mood.

Not an option she wanted to take. For someone who'd easily gone without sex for more than a year, she seemed determined to make up for lost time. She was so eager to get back to the B and

B and into Gage's arms she could probably run the entire distance back to the Upper Haight neighborhood.

But stellar sex wasn't everything. Watching Gage unwind today had made it very clear she had one more thing to do before she left Knoxville.

Someone needed to tackle the challenge of teaching him how to live before it was too late, and she was the perfect candidate. She'd been lucky enough to have a father to teach her that life was about the journey and not only the destination. There had to be more to life than just work—a concept Gage had missed if his experiences on the motorcycle and as a tourist were any indication.

The moment Gage left the boardroom late Monday morning Lauren reached for the backpack she'd tucked under the table.

They'd been hard at work for hours with Gage pushing her to test her abilities at every turn. While Gage had his wrap-up chat with the CEO she needed to get online and make her airplane payment before they packed up and headed for the airport. She hadn't done it before today because she'd needed to wait for her HAMC paycheck to clear before transferring funds, and her intention of taking care of business first thing this morning…

A chuckle rumbled from deep inside her. Well, Gage had had other plans. In the end they'd had to rush not to be late.

She closed her eyes and rested her head against the back of her chair while the computer booted up. The memory of how he'd monopolized her time flowed through her body like warm oil, tightening her nipples and creating a pool of desire in her belly.

She was exhausted and exhilarated, and she almost hated that this trip was ending. Life and the Hightowers would intrude once she and Gage touched down in Knoxville. How long would their relationship last before Trent found out and fired her?

Grimacing, she straightened, logged on to her computer and pulled up her account to transfer funds from her checking to her loan account.

Balance Due: $0.00

She frowned at the screen. That wasn't right. She still owed almost two hundred thousand dollars. She clicked on her account history. The page claimed her debt had been paid in full on Friday.

No way.

The finance company must have a software glitch or something. But she wasn't going to risk her airplane or her credit rating by skipping a payment and waiting for them to discover their error. She dug her cell phone out of her bag and dialed customer service. A recording greeted her. She hated automated machines, but typed in her account number followed by her security password when prompted. A robotic voice told her to wait for the next available operator.

She checked her watch and tried to block out the annoying elevator music pouring into her ear. Gage would be back soon and he'd be ready to leave.

"This is Rena. How can I help you today, Ms. Lynch?" a pleasant voice said.

Lauren sat up. "Hi, Rena. I'm trying to make a payment online, but there seems to be a problem with your Web page. It says my account balance is zero."

The tap of computer keys carried through the phone. "That is correct."

Lauren's heart skipped into high gear. "It can't be. I still owe your company money. A lot of money."

"No, ma'am. Your account was paid in full on Friday by certified check. Our offices will mail you the pertinent paperwork within five business days, and you can follow up with the FAA to change the ownership registry. Can I assist you with anything else today, Ms. Lynch?"

"But…that's impossible. I don't have that kind of money. Nobody I know has that kind…of… money." The words sputtered off.

Jacqui.

Her mother had to be behind this. Tension snarled in Lauren's belly and anger stiffened her spine. Gritting her teeth, she forced herself to be polite. It wasn't the customer service rep's fault that Jacqui was trying to absolve her guilt over years of ignoring her daughter with cash.

"Thank you for your help, Rena."

Lauren disconnected then immediately dialed Jacqui's cell phone. The phone rang enough times that she thought her mother was going to ignore her call again. Thanks to caller ID, Jacqui would know if the person calling was someone she wanted to talk to. And apparently, she didn't want to talk to her daughter.

Lauren was debating whether to leave yet another voice mail message when she heard, "Hello, Lauren."

How could Jacqui sound so calm? "Jacqui, did you pay off my loan?"

Silent seconds ticked past. "I wanted to help."

Anger and frustration swelled inside Lauren. Her hand clenched the phone tighter. "We've had this discussion before, and I made my feelings clear. I don't want your charity."

"But, darling—"

"I'm not your darling, Jacqui. I'm not even your daughter. Not in the way that counts. You gave me away. Save your money for your other children. Your *real* children."

She hated the anger and pain in her voice. She'd thought she'd come to terms with the knowledge of her mother's preference for her other children. Obviously not.

"Lauren, you are as much my child as they are, and they already have more than they need. You, on the other hand, are struggling to make ends meet. Your father would want me to help."

The arrow hit its target. Her father had loved this woman enough to accept whatever crumbs of affection Jacqui threw his way. Lauren didn't share that love. In fact, she realized, sometimes she almost hated Jacqui for causing her father so much pain.

"My father taught me to work for whatever I wanted and not to expect or accept handouts. I'll get a new loan as soon as I get home and pay you back."

"I won't accept your money."

Frustrated, Lauren stood and paced to the far side of the room. Why did all the Hightowers think people could be bought? Is that what being raised rich did to a person? If so, she was glad she'd missed out.

"Damn it, Jacqui, we've had this conversation too many times to count. You missed your chance to be my mother."

"And I regret that every single day. I'm sorry I let you go, Lauren."

Too little. Too late. "You know what I want from you, and I'm getting really tired of your stalling tactics. If you won't give me what I need, then I'm going back to Daytona and we're done."

A sound made her turn. Gage stood in the open doorway, his eyes narrowed. How much had he overheard? If he found out what Jacqui had done, he'd believe the worst of Lauren—the way her half siblings did. All of them would be convinced Lauren had weaseled the money out of their mother.

Lauren's stomach churned. She had to repay the loan. But could she even qualify for new financing with Falcon's current financial condition?

"We'll continue this conversation when I get back from San Francisco. I expect you to be in town and available," she told her mother and disconnected.

If you won't give me what I need then I'm going back to Daytona and we're done.

To Gage the angry words sounded like a threat. With whom had Lauren been arguing and why? And why did it bother him that she was already planning to walk away from what they had when a short-term affair had been the agenda all along? Just because they'd had two days of fantastic sex didn't mean he'd break his firm rule against permanent relationships.

His ex-wife and his mother had both bailed when they hadn't gotten their way, proving money was more important and more reliable than love. They'd cured him of ever wanting to try a permanent relationship again. But he had to thank them for the valuable lessons they'd taught him. Take what you want from a relationship and walk away.

He'd based his career on that rule. He took on a company's problems, fixed them, then moved on without a long-term commitment or a stake in the outcome. That meant there were no expectations or disappointments if those involved failed to implement his strategies.

Lauren smiled at him as she crossed the room and closed her laptop, but the curve of her lips looked strained, and her eyes lacked their usual sparkle. "All done with the CEO?"

"Yes. Problem?" He inclined his head to indicate the cell phone she held in a white-knuckle grip.

She lowered her gaze and shoved her phone into her bag. "Nothing I can't handle."

The emotional wall she'd initially kept between them had returned. He didn't like it. An unfamiliar urgency to fix whatever had upset her and get them back on a comfortable footing surged inside him like water pressure building behind a dam. "We need to eat before taking off."

"I'll order your lunch to be delivered to the

plane. That'll get us in the air faster." Tension made her movements sharp and stiff as she packed away her computer.

"You'll eat with me."

She looked ready to argue then sighed. "All right."

"In a hurry to get home?"

She slung her bag's strap over her shoulder. "It's a long flight, and we were up early. I'd rather not be too late getting back. Not to mention I'm eager to get my hands on Trent's jet again. That baby's a sweet ride. Can I help you pack your files?"

His hunger for her rekindled at the memory of waking before the alarm went off to make love to her, and then doing so again during their shared shower. Technicolor images of wet bodies, steamed glass shower doors and Lauren braced against the wall in the stall filled his brain. He blinked to clear his head, but neither the pictures nor the heat vanished.

Alarm sirens rang in his subconscious. He hadn't wanted a woman this incessantly in a very, very long time.

"I have it." He swiftly gathered his belongings, surreptitiously keeping an eye on Lauren. She shifted on her feet and stared off into space, her thoughts clearly elsewhere. "Let's go."

Lauren remained unusually silent as the CEO and his PA accompanied them to the lobby. Gage carried his end of the conversation, informing the client what to expect next in the process, but his attention was divided between the job at hand and Lauren. Women never came between him and his work, but he had to admit he'd been preoccupied with Lauren.

They said their goodbyes to the client and buckled into the rental car. Lauren stared out the window. He'd barely known her a week, but he already knew and liked the way she threw herself one hundred percent into everything she did. He liked her analytical mind, the way she relentlessly picked apart the details of an issue until she understood the big picture. Working with her had been easy because he shared the same traits. He liked that she knew how to have fun. She wasn't having any now.

He merged the car onto the highway. "The phone call upset you. What's going on?"

"Gage, it's nothing important." She pulled out her cell phone. "Excuse me for a moment. I need to call the food service people to order our meal and notify the airport that we're on our way."

Part of him admired her efficiency as she quickly dealt with preflight red tape like the pro she was, but her nonanswer frustrated him. He'd bide his time, but he would get to the bottom of what had killed her good mood before they took off.

An hour later he'd made no progress. Any attempts at private conversation had been derailed first by the need to refuel the plane and complete the ground portion of her preflight check, then once Lauren had climbed on board, the hovering staff serving their meal had made a personal discussion impossible. But finally, Lauren closed and locked the jet's door behind the departing servers, and silence filled the cabin.

Gage positioned himself so that when she turned around she stepped right into his open arms.

Her wide eyes found his. "Is something wrong?"

He rubbed her stiff back. "You tell me."

Her gaze lowered to his chin. "No. I'll have us in the air in twenty minutes."

Not if he had his way. He was determined to discover whatever had her wired, and if that meant getting her to let down her guard by stripping her out of her clothing and communicating the way they did best, then so be it. He stroked a finger along her cheek and her breathing hitched.

"Gage—" Warning filled her voice, but her pupils dilated.

"Ever made love in an airplane?"

She licked her lips. "No."

"Neither have I."

"The, um…mile high club usually waits until the plane's in the air…or so I'm told."

"I'm not interested in flying without a pilot."

"Good. Me, either. The threat of crashing isn't an aphrodisiac for me."

"Let's rock this jet, Lauren." He covered her mouth with his, savoring her soft lips, her taste, her flowery scent. A fragment of his brain wondered if he'd lost his mind. It wasn't like him to mix business with pleasure, and Lauren was definitely the latter.

Her short nails dug into his waist and the stiffness slowly drained from her. She leaned into him and her tongue twined with his as she returned the embrace. His heart pounded and desire weighted his groin.

Her palms flattened on his chest and she broke the kiss. Her cheeks were flushed, her lids heavy as she looked up at him, but passion glowed in her eyes. "This is crazy. What are we doing?"

Her breathless voice amped up his pulse rate. "We're going to put one of these leather seats to good use before we take off. As you said, once we return to Knoxville, being together will be a challenge."

She bit her lip then rested her forehead on his shoulder. "Everything will change, won't it?"

He lifted her chin and met her worried gaze. "It doesn't have to. Not yet."

But soon she'd go back to Daytona, and his life

would return to normal. The knowledge didn't fill him with the relief or satisfaction it should have. He couldn't afford to be sidetracked right now. He was too close to having Faulkner Consulting exactly where he wanted it. He had almost enough invested to make sure he'd never be homeless or go hungry again even if his business folded.

He caressed her cheek, her neck, then traced her ear. Her eyes closed and her lips parted. He kissed her again, a series of brief teasing touches of his lips on hers.

Impatient for the feel of her, the taste of her, he unbuttoned her uniform jacket then her blouse and cradled her breasts in his hands. He tugged the bra cups down until they rested beneath the swells of pale flesh, then he bent to capture one nipple in his mouth, the other with his fingers.

Her sigh filled his ears. She yanked his shirt from his pants and pressed her palms to his chest. Her hands smoothed over his back, waist and belly, inflaming him.

While he sucked and nibbled her breasts, he

outlined her hips, then slid his hands beneath her skirt to caress her incredible legs and tight, round bottom. The snug skirt restricted his movements. He worked the fabric up to her waist and peeled her panty hose and panties down for better access. His palms glided over her warm, satiny skin.

"Mmm, I love the way you touch me." Her lips teased his skin as she murmured against the side of his neck. Her hand covered his erection, and she massaged him through his pants.

Hunger racked him. A growl rumbled from deep in his gut. He wanted her *now*. He found the slick folds between her legs. Her whimper rewarded him for hitting the spot he'd learned drove her wild.

Her legs parted slightly, but she covered his hand with hers. He noted she didn't still his circling finger. "You're rushing me."

Her sexy whisper only made him more impatient to be inside her. He grazed her nipple with his teeth then lifted his head and stared into her passion-filled eyes. "This is going to be hard and fast. Got a problem with that?"

Her throaty chuckle vibrated over him. "No."

As he backed toward the nearest seat, her fingers went to work on his belt and pants. She shoved them over his butt, and he sank onto the cool leather. He stripped her panty hose and panties to her ankles then gripped her hips and pulled her toward him.

He buried his face in her curls, savoring her scent in his nose and the taste of her arousal on his tongue.

"Gage, I can't—"

"Hold on," he said against her.

She grasped his shoulders. He licked, sucked and teased her until her legs shook and her nails dug into his scalp. He kneaded her bottom with one hand and her breast with the other. Her breathing turned choppy then her back bowed. Climax shuddered through her, making her jerk against his mouth and moisten his fingers. She sagged into his hand.

He kissed her hip, tongued her navel, then her

nipples until the aftershocks passed. "I have a condom in my left pants pocket."

She leaned back in his arms, a sassy smile curving her lips. "Confident, were you?"

"I knew what we both wanted."

"Smart man. No wonder companies pay you the big bucks." She knelt in front of him and bent to dig into the trousers piled on top of the shoes he hadn't removed. Meeting his gaze, she tore the packet with her teeth and wrapped her fingers around him, but instead of rolling on the latex, she leaned forward and took him into her hot, wet mouth.

Gage slammed back against the seat as desire seared him. Her tongue swirled around the head of his shaft, and his control wavered. He gripped the armrests and fought against the explosive need building deep in his gut.

"Lauren." He growled her name in warning.

She lifted her head only a fraction. "You said you wanted fast."

Her warm breath teased his damp flesh. One of the things he liked about Lauren was she didn't play coy or try to hide her desire. She wanted him. He could see her hunger in her eyes, on her wet lips and her pink cheeks. With mischief dancing in her eyes she held his gaze, flicked her tongue over him and stroked him from base to tip and back again. He quaked with need.

"Put the damned thing on and ride me."

Her lips curved into a wicked grin. "Yes, sir. Did I mention the customer's always right?"

She taunted him by rolling on the protection slowly, rechecking the fit again and again by gliding her fingers up and down his length and cupping his nuts. The touch of her hands drove him toward the crumbling edge of his control.

"Witch."

The gutteral word made her grin widen.

He grabbed her wrists and yanked her over him. She stumbled, probably entangled in the lingerie still wound around her ankles. He caught her and urged her forward.

She planted a knee on the wide seat on either side of him. He hit the recline button, laying himself back, then guided her over his erection. She lowered, engulfing him one slow inch at a time.

A seductive smile teased her lips as she eased down until she'd taken his full length, then her breath whooshed out on a half sigh, half moan. "You feel good."

"So do you, babe. Damned good."

He lifted her skirt higher, clearing the view to watch her taking him as she rose over him, lowered, lifted again. He clutched her hips and helped her set a pace guaranteed to drive him out of his mind. Then he found her center and worked her with his thumb. Her legs trembled more with each rise and fall. His muscles clenched as he met each descent with an upward thrust.

He quickened the circles of his thumb and focused on the ecstasy chasing across her face, on the hot, slick glide of her body tightly gloving his. He was damned close, but he wasn't coming without her. Not if he could help it. He arched forward and caught a nipple between his lips.

Her orgasm hit, jerking her with the first wave. Her internal muscles contracted around him, and he quit fighting. His climax blasted from his extremities through his gut then he erupted like a geyser. Afraid he'd throw her off as the violent spasms rocked him, he grabbed her waist and held on until, drained, he dissolved into the seat.

Lauren collapsed over him with her head on his shoulder and her rapid breaths steaming his jaw. She stroked his cheek, kissed his chin. "Wow."

Her dazed tone startled a laugh out of him. He couldn't remember ever laughing during or after sex before Lauren. But he'd laughed more with her over the past few days than he had in years. She was so real, honest and upfront about her reactions.

Trent was wrong about her. Dead wrong.

"I'll second that wow." Gage caressed her moist back beneath the uniform he hadn't bothered to remove and waited for his heart and breathing to slow.

Lauren eased upright, smiling, disheveled and looking a little bemused. A lock of hair had come loose from the twist she'd pinned on the back of her head. An urge to hug her rolled over him, but he didn't do hugs. Hugs led people to expect more. He settled for tucking the silky strand behind her ear and tracing a finger over the slowing pulse at the base of her neck.

"Lauren, tell me about the phone call."

She stiffened and tried to get off him, but he clamped his hands on her thighs and held her in place.

"You're persistent, aren't you? Don't sweat it. As I've said, it's nothing I can't handle."

He didn't like being shut out. "Problem solving is what I do best. Let me help you."

She held his gaze for several moments. Indecision flickered across her face and her mouth opened then closed. She shook her head. "Not this time. But thank you for offering."

She squirmed again and he let her go. His body slipped from hers, and cool air circulating through the plane replaced her warmth, but it was her mental withdrawal that chilled him. She stood, pushed down her skirt, and turning her back, hastily pulled up her panties and hose, buttoned her shirt and straightened her uniform.

He rose and redressed while she used the onboard bathroom. When she finished he took his turn, discarding the condom and washing up. She was waiting when he returned to the cabin with her shoulders stiff and her chin high.

"I won't be distracted in the cockpit if that's what you're worried about."

"I have complete faith in your flying capabilities. If I didn't, not even Trent's friendship would make me put my life in your hands or your aircraft."

She bit her bottom lip. "I need a favor."

Tension crept into his muscles. Women always wanted something. For them, everything came with a price. "Name it."

"Please don't tell Trent about our…involvement."

"I meant it when I told you I'd keep our private business between us."

"I just needed to be sure. Thank you." She closed the distance between them, rose on tiptoe and kissed him briefly, then rocked back on her heels and took a deep breath. "Let me get this bird in the air and get us home."

She turned toward the cockpit and a heavy weight descended over him. What in the hell was his problem?

And then he knew.

He was falling for Lauren Lynch. Falling hard.

Nine

Emotion grabbed Lauren by the throat Thursday evening. The accident report fell from her shaking hands to the floor inside her apartment door where she'd torn open the package the moment the deliveryman had departed.

Grief, relief and despair twisted inside her like a waterspout. Her father's death hadn't been suicide. His crash had been caused by mechanical defect in the plane's design.

The plane she'd helped him build.

A logical corner of her mind insisted she

wasn't an aeronautical engineer, and couldn't have predicted the bolt would shear off or the disastrous results. But she'd practically been raised in a hangar. She knew aircraft structure and maintenance backward and forward, and she'd worked by her father's side on this project for the past ten years.

As many times as they'd dismantled and re-assembled the major components, why hadn't she noticed the faulty part? And how had he flown the plane so many times before without incident?

She stabbed a hand into her hair and circled the room. Maybe if he'd let her fly the plane, she'd have felt an unusual shimmy or lack of respon-siveness the failing bolt would have caused. Maybe she could have averted disaster. But her father had never let her take the controls of what he'd called his baby.

She had to call Lou. She reached for her phone, and checked her watch. No one would be in the office this late in the evening. She punched his cell number. When voice mail picked up on the first ring she groaned in frustration. He'd forgotten to turn on his phone again. She left a quick message and disconnected. For a man who could handle any technical aspect of an airplane, he hated what he called modern contraptions like cell phones. She'd only recently convinced him to use the Internet. She'd have to call him at home later after his Thursday night bowling club.

But she needed to talk to someone now, someone who would understand the contradictory guilt and relief racking her.

Gage.

The idea hit her with a jolt of adrenaline. He had a way of looking at a situation from all angles. Maybe he could help her work through the emotions torturing her. She hadn't seen him since a scowling Trent had met them the moment Lauren had opened the airplane door Monday night, and strangely enough, she'd missed Gage the past three days.

Had what they'd shared in San Francisco meant nothing to him? Had he decided to dump her now that he'd slept with her? The idea hurt, and that was stupid because there was no chance of a future between them. But still…

She'd thought him different from the Whits of this world who used a woman then moved on as soon as a model with better perks and more connections came along. If she hadn't, she never would have gone to bed with Gage.

Either way, she didn't want to call him. Because of his connection to Trent, revealing the financial reasons some believed her father had committed suicide wouldn't be a good idea. Falcon's indebtedness would only reinforce every negative belief her half siblings had about her.

That left Jacqui—if Jacqui was back in the country. She hadn't been home when Lauren returned from San Francisco. But Jacqui wasn't a good choice since she was rarely the voice of reason. Still…as much as Lauren had been haranguing her mother for answers, Jacqui deserved to know what the report had uncovered.

Lauren grabbed the papers and her keys and raced down the stairs to her truck. The bite of the cold night air penetrated her sweater, making her realize she'd forgotten her coat. Too bad. She wasn't taking the time to go back and fetch it.

Shivering, she revved the engine and headed for the Hightower estate. If she was lucky, Trent wouldn't be there. Twenty minutes later she hit the doorbell.

Fritz opened the door. "Good evening, Miss Lynch."

"Is she here?"

"In the salon."

"Is Trent here?"

"No, miss."

Good.

Fritz turned and led the way. "Ms. Lynch, for you, Madam."

He stepped aside, revealing Jacqui sitting near the fireplace, dressed immaculately as always, this time in a dark teal color that brought out the color of her eyes. Lauren couldn't remember ever seeing her mother looking less than perfect. Jacqui's perfection had always been daunting for a rough-and-tumble girl who'd usually had skinned knees, scraped knuckles and hair trimmed by her father.

"Lauren, this is a surprise." Jacqui rose and crossed the room to give her one of those meaningless air kisses.

"I'm sorry I didn't call. I'm surprised Fritz let me in."

"He's been told I'm always available to you."

Nice, but a couple of decades too late. And being physically available didn't equate to being emotionally accessible. "I have the accident report. Dad's death wasn't suicide."

"I told you it wasn't." Jacqui seemed even more tense than her usual uptight self.

"But why should I have believed you when you wouldn't tell me anything else? Like what you and Daddy discussed that afternoon that sent him racing for the airstrip the moment you left. He flew off without filing a flight plan or telling anyone where he was going or when he'd be back."

"That's because I—" Jacqui looked away briefly. "I'm sorry. May I offer you some refreshment?"

Lauren gritted her teeth over the stalling tactic.

Jacqui had quite a varied collection of ways to avoid a discussion. "No. Thank you. If we'd known his flight plan, he wouldn't have lain out there in the Glades so long."

Jacqui flinched. "The medical examiner's report stated Kirk died instantly and didn't suffer while waiting for rescue."

"That's the only thing that makes the idea of him dying alone bearable."

Jacqui squared her narrow shoulders as if bracing herself. "What did the report say?"

Words tumbled in Lauren's head—words a nonpilot wouldn't understand. "Without getting technical, the plane's design was faulty. There was too much stress on some parts. Dad hit stall speed during a steep turn and lost control because a bolt sheared off. He was flying too close to the ground to level out and set her down on her belly. That's why he went in wing first."

Jacqui bowed her head, covered her mouth with one beringed, manicured hand and turned away. A muffled sob broke the silence then her shoulders shook.

Watching her mother's grief made Lauren uncomfortable. Unsure of what to do, she picked at the side seam of her jeans and cleared her tightening throat.

Pilots don't cry. Her father's voice echoed in her head.

She inhaled deeply, struggled for composure. *Focus on the facts.* "I should have noticed the worn part when we broke the plane down and re-assembled her. If I had, then maybe he'd still be with us."

Jacqui spun around, fists curled, body taut. Her mother's red-rimmed eyes zeroed in on her. "Don't you dare blame yourself for this. You have nothing to feel guilty about. *I* am the one who should have stopped him."

Lauren blinked in surprise at her mother's vehement tone. "How do you think you could have done that?"

"If I hadn't given him the money—" Another sob choked off her words, leaving nothing but the crackle of the fire to fill the silence.

Lauren senses went on alert. "Money for what?"

Jacqui wrung her hands. "The engineering evaluation, the repeated upfittings…"

A knot formed in Lauren's stomach. "Wait a minute. Back up. What engineering evaluation?"

Jacqui's fidgeting stopped. "Kirk didn't tell you?"

"Tell me what?"

Her mother crossed to the wet bar and splashed clear liquor from a crystal decanter into a matching tumbler. After taking a healthy swig, she faced Lauren.

"Kirk contacted me just before your eighteenth birthday. He had designed an airplane that he was sure was going to make him rich. He knew there was something not quite right with it, but didn't know what or how to fix the problem. He asked me to use my connections to get an independent engineering consult. I agreed on the condition that I got to tell you I was your mother and spend more time with you. I had wanted to for years, but that wasn't part of my original agreement with your father or my husband."

Lauren let the information soak in. Her mother

had wanted to see her? She found that hard to believe. "About the money…?"

"Your father couldn't afford the engineer's fee. I had chosen the best, of course. So I paid it." She paused to gulp more of her drink. "The engineer found a flaw in the swept-back wing design and told your father it couldn't be corrected. It was something intrinsic in the structure. In fact, the engineer recommended your father not continue to fly the plane. But that airplane was your father's dream, and he wouldn't be dissuaded. He convinced me to loan him the money to keep working on the design. Because I couldn't bear to kill his enthusiasm, I continued to fund the project."

Maybe her half siblings had good reason to distrust her. "How much money are we talking here?"

"That's irrelevant. It was my money to do with as I pleased, and until recently, I covered my tracks well."

"What do you mean *until recently?*"

"Trent's minions have been spying on me. They reported my recent transactions."

No wonder her brother hated her. But she'd deal with that later. "Back to Dad and that day."

"What sent your father off that afternoon was me. *Me.*" Jacqui's voice cracked. "I asked him to give up, to admit defeat. I did so, not because of the money, but because I was afraid for him. He kept pushing that airplane harder and harder, trying to prove the engineer wrong. And then Kirk admitted he couldn't afford to quit. He needed to sell and patent the plane's design to cover his debts."

Light-headed, Lauren gripped the back of a chair. Her father had known the plane was faulty and chosen to risk his life anyway. For money. Did everything always come down to money?

"Why didn't you tell me this sooner?"

"Because if I hadn't encouraged him, he'd still be alive. Don't hate me, Lauren. I did what I did because I loved him. I wanted him to be happy."

Lauren shook her head in disbelief. "You funded a suicide mission. That's a strange way to show your love."

A mixture of anger and grief toward this

woman and toward her father churned in her belly. "It's likely that he turned to you because he'd already borrowed as much as he possibly could against Falcon Air. We're maxed out. And with the economic downturn of the past few years, business has decreased. We've been struggling to make the payments on his loans.

"If the life insurance company finds out he flew against the engineer's recommendation, they might call his death an act of willful negligence and refuse to pay. And then Falcon will be in deep trouble. We'll have to file bankruptcy or find a buyer."

"I'll give you whatever you need."

The idea repulsed her. "I don't want your money, Jacqui. I've never wanted your money. And what I want now, you can't give me."

"Tell me what it is and I'll find a way," Jacqui pleaded.

"I want my father back."

Lauren had never been one to run away from her problems, but at the moment she ached to be in the cockpit of her Cirrus high above the clouds or racing down the highway on her Harley with the wind tearing at her hair.

She knew better than to operate either machine with her concentration shattered, which was why she was sitting on the side of the road in her pickup staring at the streetlight and trying to gather her composure.

With hindsight, she wished she hadn't pulled over to answer her cell phone when Lou had returned her call because she was too angry to be tactful.

"You knew," she choked out.

Silence stretched through the airwaves. "Yeah, I knew," Lou finally responded.

It was bad enough that her father and mother had selfishly pursued a death wish, but Lou, too? And they'd all kept the engineer's report from her. Hurt and betrayal burned through her.

"Lauren, your dad was a genius with airplanes. I believed Kirk could find a way to reduce the stress on the wing and fix the problem. If anyone could, he could."

Lauren's hands shook so badly she nearly dropped the phone. "But the *expert* said it wasn't fixable."

"And we both know what your daddy did when somebody told him he couldn't do something. He set out to prove 'em wrong. Same as you'd do. You may be the spittin' image of your momma, but you're your daddy's girl through and through. You got his grit, his flying skills and you sure as hell got his mule-headed stubbornness."

She made a face at the phone. It wasn't the first time she'd been accused of being…persistent. But she didn't see that as a fault. "I would never die just to prove a point."

"He didn't do it on purpose, Lauren."

Her father's death seemed like a senseless waste, an avoidable accident. "Didn't anybody care what *I* thought about him risking his life?"

"He didn't think it was a risk. He'd already logged a hundred hours on that plane before he had the engineer look at it."

"Turns out he was wrong. Lou, I gotta go."

Before she did something stupid like bawl her eyes out.

Pilots don't cry.

Heart aching, Lauren disconnected. She couldn't go back to her empty apartment, and she couldn't keep driving aimlessly around Knoxville.

Gage. Gage would help her put this into perspective.

To hell with what her siblings thought. If her father's life insurance refused to pay up, Falcon's financial woes would be in the airline news soon anyway when its assets went on the auction block.

Gage's muscles ached with fatigue, and his eyes felt as if someone had dumped a bag of sand into them. Spending the past thirty-six hours without sleep by his father's side had left him wanting food, a hot shower and a comfortable bed.

He considered ignoring whoever was ringing his doorbell, but he still had a business to run. He'd been incommunicado since his cell phone battery died two days ago, and he'd forgotten to check the message machine when he'd dragged himself into the house.

The smell of the hospital still clung to him, but he reached into the glass cubicle of his shower and shut off the inviting steamy spray. He dragged on a bathrobe and slowly descended the stairs to his foyer. Who would be visiting at almost midnight? He checked the peephole.

Lauren. His heart jolted into a faster rhythm. He hadn't spoken to her since Trent had greeted him at the airport with news of his father's hospitalization. Afterward, while his father had lain in intensive care hovering between life and death, calling anyone had never crossed his mind.

His exhaustion vanished. His formerly leaded limbs suddenly felt lighter. He opened the door.

With her arms wrapped around her middle, she stood shivering and pale on his porch without a coat. Her hair was disheveled and a worried pleat creased her brow. She didn't look like she'd been resting during her days off.

She stared up at him. "I'm sorry. I know it's late, but can I come in?"

"Of course." Because he wanted so badly to take her into his arms, he stepped out of the way instead. She passed by, leaving a hint of flowers in the air. He closed the door. She shifted on her feet looking ill at ease. "What's wrong, Lauren?"

"I received the accident report on my father's crash today, and I…I need you to help me make sense of it."

Having been through hell and back with his father in the past few days, her unusual vulnerability pulled at something familiar deep in his chest. He took her hand in his. Her fingers were as cold as ice. He led her to his den. A flick of a switch ignited the gas logs. He sat on an ottoman in front of the fireplace and pulled her down beside him.

A shudder racked her. He put his arm around her shoulders and pulled her close. The action felt eerily natural and comfortable. She pressed her face into the open V of his robe. The shock of her cold cheek against his skin contrasted with the warmth of her breath on his flesh. Thoughts of bed returned, this time not involving the eight hours of uninterrupted sleep he needed. But sex wasn't what Lauren needed right now. And hell, as tired as he was, he wasn't sure he was capable. A humbling thought.

He rubbed her stiff back. "What did the report say?"

"My father didn't commit suicide. At least not intentionally."

Unintentional suicide didn't compute. "Explain."

"He—*we*—built an experimental aircraft, my father, Lou and me. Dad planned to patent the design and sell it. But—" she inhaled shakily "—the design was flawed. Dad knew it. My mother knew it. Even my uncle knew. But Dad flew the stupid plane anyway. He pushed it beyond its limits…and it killed him."

Her words echoed his concerns about his own father who seemed hell-bent on following a dream regardless of the costs. "Go on."

"Gage, I spent almost as many hours working on that plane as he did. I should have seen the flaw."

Self-blame. Another familiar refrain. He understood and had experienced the same helpless frustration numerous times. His determination to fix his father's life had caused a rift between him and his dad that seemed unbridgeable. They'd barely spoken in the past few years.

"Lauren, the accident wasn't your fault."

Her eyes beseeched him, and he wanted to sweep in like a superhero and fix her problems.

"He never asked what *I* wanted. I would much rather have my father alive and with me than have a damned airplane named after me. I'm a better pilot. If he'd let me fly it—"

A crushing sensation settled on his chest. "Then you might be dead instead of him. My father also has an apparent death wish, and he's more than willing to die for what he believes in. Helping others might sound like an admirable goal, but not at the risk of his personal safety.

"I realized years ago that I can't control him. Not that I haven't tried. But he's not a child. What he does is not my fault. The best I can do is be around to pick up the pieces."

She leaned back, her eyes brimming with questions. "What happened?"

He hadn't intended to share his past with her, but he'd already shared more with Lauren than anyone else except Trent. And Trent only knew because he'd lived through some of it with Gage. An urgent need for her to know who he was and where he'd come from rose within him.

"I told you I lived in the family car for a while." He waited for her nod. "Before that my father was a successful real estate developer. His dreams were always larger than life, and we lived the high life. Not on the Hightowers' level, but close. By the time I turned ten he'd overextended himself, taking on more debt than he could handle. Then the real estate market tanked. He hadn't prepared for that, and he lost everything, including our home. We lived in the family car for six months. My mother bailed after three.

"Dad never regained the drive to try again. We were in and out of public housing projects and shelters after that because he couldn't hold a job. He wasn't cut out for taking orders or being anyone's subordinate. He was too used to being the boss."

The sympathy in Lauren's eyes almost dammed his words. "What about your mother?"

He shrugged. "I never saw her again and haven't looked for her."

"Not knowing you is her loss, Gage." Her fingers squeezed his. "Is your father still alive?"

"Not for lack of trying to kill himself. Seven years ago I bought him a house, but he insists on hanging out at the local homeless shelter. He claims he's found his true calling in helping others.

"It's a rough inner-city crowd, and Dad doesn't hesitate to step in when fights break out. He's been hurt a few times, but this week—" Knowing how close he'd come to losing his father made his throat close up. "This week he tried to break up a knife fight and got sliced up. By the time I reached the hospital he'd already flatlined once, but they'd brought him back. I've been there since we landed."

"That's why Trent was waiting for us—for you?"

"Yes. Tonight they moved Dad out of intensive care. He's going to pull through. That's the only reason I came home. For a shower and some sleep."

"Gage, I'm sorry." Her sincerity shone in her eyes and his lungs took a siesta. He wasn't used to someone caring for him. And then he realized he'd never allowed anyone to. He'd kept his acquaintances at a distance and never let them see behind the wall he'd built around himself. Only Lauren had blasted through, by refusing to back off when he threw up barricades.

Head reeling at the discovery, he tried to remember his point. "I wish I could believe this would teach Dad a lesson, but it won't. Lauren, our parents make choices over which we have no control. You can't beat yourself up over it. You have to let them live their lives the same way you want them to let you live yours."

Her wide gaze held his and he saw acceptance slowly seep in followed by gratitude then regret. She mentally pulled away before she stiffened in his arms. "Thank you for helping me make sense of this. I should get out of here and let you rest."

The idea of her leaving repelled him. "Stay."

"You need sleep."

"I need you more." The minute the words left his mouth he knew they were true. After seeing his father's failure and his mother's and ex-wife's fickle natures, Gage had sworn he'd never allow himself to need anyone again. But Lauren made him want more than just a financially secure future. She made him want someone to share it with.

And allowing himself to want something he couldn't control scared the crap out of him.

Ten

The warmth of the fire at Lauren's back couldn't compare to the heat in Gage's eyes. Her heart blipped wildly and her mouth moistened as Gage lowered his head.

His lips swept hers so tenderly, emotion welled up in her throat. Choking back a sob, she broke the kiss, buried her face in his neck and wrapped her arms around his middle, hugging him as tightly as she could.

Gage soothed her with long strokes down her spine and soft kisses in her hair, on her temple, along her jaw. The tumultuous feelings inside her morphed into something altogether different, and by the time his mouth returned to hers, Lauren ached for him and for the passion and momentary oblivion he could offer.

She tunneled her fingers into the opening of his robe, gliding her hands over his warm, supple skin and savoring each hiss of his breath. She wasn't supposed to feel this close to him, this emotionally bonded to him. He was supposed to be temporary, a plane that passed in the night-dark sky.

He rose, pulling her to her feet, then with one powerful kick he sent the ottoman skidding out of the way. He peeled away her clothing with economical precision. Her sweater, bra, pants and panties landed in a pile on the floor. He stepped back, his eyes devouring her as he stripped off his robe and spread it on the rug in front of the fire.

He scooped her into his arms, startling a gasp out of her and knelt to gently lay her on his robe. Thick velour fabric cushioned her back. Seconds later his hot body blanketed her front, before he slid to her side, freeing his hands to map her body with devastating, bone-melting thoroughness.

In the past they'd made love feverishly, but this time Gage lingered, painting languorous circles over her breasts, belly and thighs alternately with his palms and fingertips, making her core shudder with every pass closer and closer to her center.

Hungry for him, she captured his face in her hands and brought his mouth back to hers. His tongue plunged in, sweeping, stroking. His fingers mimicked the action, delving into her curls, finding her moisture, caressing her most sensitive spot until her back bowed as pleasure twined ever tighter inside her.

She tore her mouth away to gasp and grip his shoulders as release shuddered through her like the rise and fall of turbulence, and then drained, she melted into the floor.

He pulled her into his arms and soothed her with gentle kisses. She forced her heavy lids open. Banked hunger still raged in his eyes and in the erection pressing to her hip, but he made no move to drive inside her the way she wanted him to.

"Your turn." She tried to push him onto his back, but he resisted.

He brushed his lips over hers. "This time was all about you, baby."

She stroked her fingertips down his chest until she reached the rigid flesh between them and coiled her hand around him. "Gage, let me make you feel as good as you made me."

He caressed her face. "You do that by being here."

Her heart and lungs contracted as if a giant fist had squeezed them, and Lauren knew she was in trouble.

This wasn't just about sex or two people finding comfort and pleasure in each other.

She'd fallen in love with Gage Faulkner.

Run, run home to Daytona. You have your answers. Now you can go.

She mentally dug in her heels, even though she'd already lived through the rich man–working girl scenario once before and knew a happy ending was unlikely. The ugly finish of her relationship with Whit had nearly broken her, and she hadn't felt nearly as connected to him as she did to Gage. That had been a Cinderella fantasy.

This…this was love. And it was terrifying and exhilarating. And she was not going to run from it.

Her life was a mess. She had no business dragging Gage into it. But if she wanted even a slim chance of a future with him, she had to tell him the whole truth, and hope he believed her and not Trent's poison. And maybe if she was very, *very* lucky, Gage would help her find a way to save Falcon Air.

She opened her mouth, but the words wouldn't come out. She wouldn't tell him, not tonight. Tonight he was tired, and she wanted to sleep in his arms knowing she loved him.

Tomorrow would be soon enough to find out if he was going to break her heart.

Gage absently stirred the eggs while he tried to figure out what about the way he and Lauren had made love this morning bothered him. The prolonged episode, while still hot and extremely satisfying, had felt like a goodbye.

Everything in him rejected the idea. He wasn't going to let her go. Lauren tormented and tested him, but she'd also made him feel more alive than he had in years. Having her in bed beside him when he'd awoken this morning had felt *right*—like a habit to which he would like to become accustomed.

How could he make it work when her life was in Daytona and his business was here? It would be business suicide for her to move Falcon Air onto Hightowers' home field. But he'd worked long and hard to build a Faulkner Consulting team he could trust. He wouldn't break them apart. The past few weeks had proven that with a jet and a pilot on call he could get anywhere faster. Would a long-distance affair last?

"Gage," Lauren called from behind him. The quiver of her voice caused the fine hairs on his nape to prickle with unease. "There's something I need to tell you."

He knew before he turned off the burner and faced her that whatever she had to say would likely blow his good mood to smithereens.

She hovered near the entrance of his breakfast area, her long legs bare beneath the hem of one of his white T-shirts. He could see the shadows of her areolas and the points of her nipples through the fabric. Desire pulsed in his groin even though he'd made love to her barely an hour ago.

Worry clouded her eyes and furrowed her forehead. He nodded, indicating she continue.

"I learned more from my mother than about my father's crash." She pleated the hem of his shirt between her fingers, flashing him glimpses of her upper thigh.

He forced his gaze from her sexy legs to her face. "Go on."

"Please hear me out before you jump to conclusions."

The burn in his stomach intensified.

"Jacqui has been funding my father for years, beginning with paying for the aeronautical engineering study then for improvements to the plane."

That answered Trent's question about where the money had been going. "How much?"

"I don't know exactly. She wouldn't say. And then…" She bit her lip and glanced away. Her breasts rose and fell on a deep in- and exhalation before her cautious gaze returned to his. He braced himself.

"She paid off my airplane loan."

Her words hit him like a sucker punch. The missing two hundred grand.

"I found out while we were in San Francisco when I tried to make my payment online."

If you won't give me what I need, then I'm going back to Daytona and we're done.

Lauren had been furious and insistent with the person on the other end of the phone. Looked as if she'd gotten her way, and her way was little better than extortion.

"Gage, I didn't ask her to pay it."

He didn't believe her. He'd heard the argument.

"I've told her a hundred times that I don't want her money. I've never wanted her frilly dresses or dumb dolls or useless manicures. All I wanted was a mother who'd braid my hair, kiss my boo-boos and teach me about boys and makeup. Things money can't buy. And all I wanted when I came to Knoxville was answers. Until last night she withheld those."

Her words gushed like water from a broken mainline, pouring over each other in a tumbled rush. Was she protesting too much? In his line of work he'd learned that those with something to hide always gave more information than the situation required. They talked fast and avoided eye contact—exactly the way Lauren was doing now.

"I intend to get a loan and pay her back. If I can. But—"

"But what, Lauren?"

She fidgeted uneasily with fussy fingers, wiggly toes, shifting shoulders. "Falcon Air is in trouble. Before my father approached Jacqui for money, he borrowed heavily against the company to finance building his plane. If the insurance company finds out he knew the plane was faulty and chose to fly it even though he'd been warned against it by the engineer, they may not pay. If that happens, I might lose Falcon Air…" Her pleading gaze met his. "Unless you'll help me."

He recoiled. Trent had been right. Lauren had been trying to get her hooks into the Hightower fortune. Gage felt like a fool for once again being taken in by a woman's lies.

What was his problem? A little sexual attraction and his brain ceased to function? He'd be damned if he'd let her humiliate him the way Angela had—Angela, who'd strung him along with her professed adoration, her duplicitous nature and her betrayal.

"What you're telling me is you and your father have been milking Jacqueline for cash for years, and now you want to tap into me, too."

She paled. "No. *No.* I want your business consulting expertise to help me turn Falcon around. I've seen you work, Gage. I know you can do it."

"You want to hire me?"

She bit her lip. "I'm not sure I can afford you. But I'm sure we can work out something."

"Like what? Sex for services rendered?"

She flinched and then her chin lifted and her shoulders squared. "How can you say that?"

"Seems obvious. You want something from me, and you're willing to sleep with me to get it."

Dots of angry color appeared on her cheeks. "I was trying to barter with you in a way that would benefit us both. I was thinking more along the lines of trading my piloting skills for your business acumen. You need to travel. I have a plane. I want to save my company and the jobs of all Falcon's employees. Gage, I don't want your money. You have to believe me. I love you."

A jolt from a defibrillator would hurt less. The pain jarred his body. Her declaration was a perfect example that women would say and do anything to get what they wanted. How many times had his ex sworn she loved him? How many times had he looked into her eyes and believed her lies? How many times had he been a fool?

And then Angela and her lawyers had screwed him over. He'd almost lost Faulkner Consulting.

As it was, she'd stripped him of every liquid asset he had, and he'd had to start rebuilding the security he'd worked so damned hard for from scratch because of her greed.

But he wanted to believe Lauren, ached to believe her, and his weakness disgusted him. "No."

"No? That's it? No?"

"You're on your own. I no longer need a pilot or you. Goodbye, Lauren. You know your way out."

She stared at him for ten full seconds, her bottom lip quivering until she caught it between her teeth, then she turned and staggered from the room. He was a little surprised she didn't argue. He had to fight the compulsion to go after her as he listened to her climb the stairs then descend moments later. The front door opened then closed. Lauren's big V-10 engine roared in the driveway then the sound faded away.

He congratulated himself on averting another disastrous mercenary relationship.

But the relief he'd expected to feel was nowhere in sight.

* * *

Lauren stared at the life insurance check in her hand and recounted the zeroes.

She looked up at her uncle Lou. "This is enough to pay off everything Dad borrowed against Falcon Air and give us a nice cushion. Our financial problems are solved."

So why didn't she feel better?

"Hallelujah. Now if we can get your personal problems fixed, we'll be right as rain."

She stiffened. She thought she'd done a better job of hiding her broken heart by diving right in and assuming her dad's old duties in addition to hers. "I don't have any problems."

"Bull. You've been moping around here for three weeks. If your face gets any longer you'll run over your bottom lip with your landing gear."

"I'm pulling my weight."

"Yes, baby girl, you are. But like the sign behind you says, 'Making a living is not the same as making a life.'" He pointed to the sign hanging on the wall behind her father's—now her desk. "You're running on autopilot and logging too many hours. I'm guessing you have unfinished business back in Knoxville. And I don't mean with your momma."

"Then you'd be guessing wrong. Without trust you have nothing. And that's what I left in Knoxville. Nothing." Too bad her heart hadn't signed off on that plan.

She rubber-stamped the back of the check with For Deposit Only then rose and gathered her gear. "I have a lesson to teach. Send Joey out to the Cirrus when he gets here."

She slapped Lou in the belly with the check as she passed. "Take this to the bank when you leave for lunch."

"Lauren, it hurts me to see you like this."

Lou's gruff, but gentle voice stopped her in the doorway. Her aching heart swelled for love of this man. He and Falcon Air were all she had left. "Don't sweat it, Lou. It's like a cold. I'll get over it."

She pivoted and strode out of the office. Her stupid stinging eyes started watering again. Damn Florida's fall grass and weed pollen.

She shoved on her sunglasses then walked around her newly refinanced airplane, doing her preflight check even though she knew she'd make her student repeat the process. The routine soothed her.

As soon as she'd returned from Knoxville, she'd applied for a new loan. When the loan had come through last week she'd mailed a check to Trent with a brief explanation because she'd known her mother wouldn't accept her money. Her half brother hadn't bothered to reply. Said a lot about what he thought of her. But that was just as well. She wanted nothing to do with the Hightowers, either.

Tomorrow when the life insurance check cleared, she'd pay off the rest of Falcon's debts, and she'd once again be free and clear except for the Cirrus.

Life was good.

So why didn't it feel like it?

The last time Gage had found Trent waiting for him outside on the tarmac at the bottom of the airplane stairs, the news his friend had delivered hadn't been good. Judging by Trent's drawn face and tight lips, what he had to say today wasn't going to be any better.

Whatever the current catastrophe might be, Gage wasn't sure he had the energy to deal with it. In the three and a half weeks since Lauren had left, he'd been running around the clock. He worked and slept, woke and showered on an airplane, then reported to the client's office only to begin the entire process again on the flight to the next destination. He couldn't go back to his empty house without picturing Lauren on the rug in front of his fireplace or in his bed.

Trent stood by silently as Gage descended the stairs and thanked today's crew for a good flight. When Gage returned his attention to Trent, his friend held a slip of paper in his extended hand. Curious, Gage took it.

His bleary eyes scanned a certified check for two hundred thousand dollars made out to Trent Hightower, then he zeroed in on the signature of the payer. Lauren Lynch.

A burst of adrenaline kicked up his heart rate. A cold knot formed in Gage's gut and a heavy weight landed on his shoulders. "What's this?"

Trent's exhaled breath clouded the frigid air between them. "Lauren sent the check with a note saying our mother would never cash it, but she trusted me to handle getting the funds back where they belonged. And she promised to make payments of a thousand a month on the remainder of the money our mother gave her father over the past seven years. It's a substantial sum."

Thoughts slammed around Gage's head. His tired brain couldn't begin to sort them out or even find a starting point to making reparation.

"You okay?" Trent asked when Gage said nothing.

He'd been wrong about Lauren. "I was afraid to trust her or the power of what she made me feel. I called her a liar and ordered her out of my house, believing she'd screwed me over the same way Angela had by lying and setting me up to bleed me dry. Instead, I'm the one who wronged her. How in the hell can I apologize for that?"

"Wait a minute. You and Lauren? You never said anything."

"It was none of your business." He raked a hand over his gritty eyes while guilt burned in his stomach like acid. "I treated her badly."

Trent grunted. "You're not the only one. I thought she was a money-sucking leech. I perceived her as a threat, and I did everything I could to run her off. Bottom-of-the-barrel jobs. Obnoxious clients. Our worst planes. Hell, any other employee would have sued me for harassment.

"Mom's a hysterical mess because Lauren's refusing to take her calls. She's threatened to fly down to Daytona, but Lauren's uncle warned her she wouldn't be welcome and that he'd have her escorted off the property."

Gage knew Lauren had to be hurting to take such drastic measures.

"I love her. Lauren. Not your mother." The words burst out before he could stop them.

For the first time in Gage's memory, Trent looked flabbergasted. "Shit. You should have said something."

"I have to find a way to fix this. I can fix this. Fixing things is what I do. And I'm good at it." Who in the hell was he trying to convince? He'd be lucky if Lauren didn't throw him headfirst into a spinning propeller.

He deserved it.

Trent clapped a hand on Gage's shoulder. "My jet is the fastest one we own. It's yours whenever you want it."

"How about now?"

Trent startled and glanced at his watch. "It'll take me a couple of hours to find a pilot."

"What about Phil?" He jerked his thumb over his shoulder to indicate the man who'd just flown him back from Seattle.

"He's maxed out on his hours in the air for the week."

"You fly me."

Trent shrank back. "I haven't taken the controls in twelve years. I'm not risking both our necks."

"C'mon Trent, Lauren says that plane practically flies itself."

"Flying's not like driving a car, Gage. You can't just climb back into the cockpit. All the computerized components are different. Lauren just lost her father to a plane crash. I'm not costing her you, too. Besides, my plane's too damned pretty to break."

The last was clearly a forced attempt at humor. Gage swallowed his objections. "Find me a pilot. Get me to Daytona."

"You've got it. Now go home and clean up. You look like a mangy dog. She won't let you in the house if you show up like that."

Eleven

Lauren's senses went on alert when an unexpected aircraft turned from Daytona International's taxi runway onto the ramp in front of Falcon's hangars.

Her stomach did a loop-de-loop and her pulse stuttered when she identified the make and model as a Sino Swearingen SJ30-2. Her half brother's plane.

No. Couldn't be.

Her gaze shot to the tail number, hoping she was wrong. Her mood nosedived at the familiar sequence she'd relayed into the radio when she'd flown the jet. Her anger stirred.

Trent Hightower had invaded Falcon territory.

What did *he* want? She knew he'd received the check four days ago because she'd sent it by registered mail and he'd signed for it.

The jet came to a stop. She didn't want to talk to him. On second thought, she wouldn't mind if he'd flown to Daytona to apologize and grovel. Especially grovel. The jerk.

Or maybe it was her mother. She didn't want to talk to her, either. They had nothing left to say.

"Sweet ride," her student said. "One of Falcon's?"

She forced her brain back into instructor mode. "No. Check the call sign. All of our N-Numbers end in *FA* for Falcon Air. That one's *HA*, registered to Hightower Aviation. Let's finish your postflight inspection. Where are you on your checklist?"

Her student returned to his task, but he was as distracted by the flashy jet as Lauren. Her ears picked up every sound from behind her, but she kept her eyes focused on her beloved Cirrus. She heard the trespassing aircraft's parking break engage and involuntarily cataloged each step of proper shutdown procedure thereafter.

When the jet's door opened her spine went rigid, but she didn't turn around. If Trent wanted to talk to her, he'd have to cool his jets—the way he'd made her wait outside his office so many times.

When she couldn't stall any longer she signed off on her student's logbook. "That's it for today. You did well. Study for your solo flight next week, and don't forget to wear a shirt I can cut off you. I don't want your mom screaming at me for ruining your best dress shirt."

The postsolo shirt-cutting ceremony was the highlight of her students' lessons. Hers, too. Most of the shirttails hanging on the hangar walls of Falcon's office had come from her students.

"Cool. Can't wait." The seventeen-year-old almost skipped away, leaving Lauren with a memory of having once been that carefree back in the day when she didn't know about debts or her other family—one of which had decided to curse her with a visit.

Taking a bracing breath she pivoted to face her unwelcome relative. Gage stood beside the open cabin door. Gage. Not Trent. Her muscles seized. She couldn't breathe, couldn't move.

Dark sunglasses shielded his eyes, but that thick, glossy dark hair, perfectly shaped body and his purposeful stride were unmistakable. He wore his leather motorcycle jacket unzipped over a black T-shirt, jeans and his black biker boots. Her pulse got as wild as a Mardi Gras parade.

Why was he here? Dressed like that. And where was his obnoxious sidekick? She glanced past Gage to the plane but only saw one of HAMC's pilots circling the aircraft doing his postflight. No sneering half brother waited in the plane's open door.

Her gaze ricocheted back to Gage only thirty feet away and closing, his heels hitting the concrete with a brisk pace. Lauren's heart hammered. Her mouth dried and her hands moistened. With colossal effort, she rallied her anger. His lack of trust had cut deeply. She'd given him her heart, and he'd given her the boot.

Hugging the clipboard to her chest, she wished she could come up with a snarky insult. But her brain refused to cough up any witty words, so she remained mute.

Gage stopped a yard away. "Hello, Lauren."

His deep voice tugged at something buried inside her. She nodded. "Gage."

"We need to talk."

Right. So he could insult her some more? Tear another chunk out of her heart and crush it beneath his shoes? Nope. "I'm working."

"Tell me a convenient time. I'll come back."

Wow. That didn't sound like him. He was usually pushier. "Never sounds pretty good."

He took a quick breath and ripped off his sunglasses. The pain and regret in his dark eyes made her gasp. "I'm prepared to camp on your ramp until you and I have talked."

"Go home, Gage. You're wasting your time." She had to get away from him. The pollen was burning her eyes again. She turned toward the office.

"I have something for you."

She stopped. He held out an envelope. She kept her arms folded over the clipboard.

"It's from Trent."

Probably her final paycheck. She wouldn't have been surprised if her butt-headed half brother had refused to pay her, since she'd left HAMC without working out her two weeks' notice. Since landing in Daytona she'd tried to work up a little guilt over that, but she'd failed. Trent had wanted her gone, and in her opinion, she'd done him a favor by granting his wish.

But hey, if he wanted to throw money at her to ease his conscience for being a prick, she'd take it and donate it to the local Bikers Against Drunk Driving fund. She plucked the envelope from Gage's fingers, tore it open and pulled out the check inside.

A cashier's check for two hundred thousand dollars shook in her hand. Her check. Uncashed. She shoved the paper back where it had come from and thrust the envelope back at Gage. "This isn't mine."

He made no move to take it. "Trent says it is. Either you use the money to pay off your new loan, or I'm to shred the check in front of you. Either way, Trent says to tell you he's not cashing it."

"He can't do that."

A smile twitched one corner of that delectable mouth. "Trent can do pretty much whatever he wants. Most of your Hightower siblings can. Get used to it. You're one of them now."

"I am not. So you're acting as his delivery boy now?"

Gage's lips compressed. "I offered to return your money, since I was coming down anyway."

She scanned his clothing. "Bike week's in March."

"I'm not here for bike week. I'm here for you."

Her lungs did that lockdown thing they usually did when he touched her—only this time he stood a yard away. "Too bad. Because I'm not available to you."

She did an about-face and hustled toward the

hangar. His footsteps followed, deliberate and firm. "Lauren, I made a mistake."

"That's not news," she called over her shoulder without slowing.

"I'm here to help you save Falcon Air. And if I can't come up with a revitalization strategy, then I'll become a silent investor."

Not knowing what to make of his declaration or whether to trust it, she slowly turned. "Thanks, but I no longer need your help. Dad's life insurance paid up. Falcon is back in the black. Besides, you should know by now that I'm no one's charity case. I pay my way."

"Then maybe you'll help me."

What was he trying to pull? "With what?"

"I'm looking for property in the area, and I don't know my way around."

"A vacation home?"

"Two properties. The first is commercial. I'm relocating Faulkner Consulting to Daytona. The second is residential. I put my house on the market."

Her mouth dried. Whatever game he was

playing, she didn't have time for it. She resumed her path to the office. He kept pace beside her. She glanced at him. "What's the matter? Knoxville's cold weather getting to you?"

A smile eased over his lips and the gold flecks in his eyes glittered with warmth. "No. I fell for a Harley-riding pilot chick. She lives here."

Lauren tripped over the threshold and would have fallen flat on her face if Gage hadn't caught her arm and hauled her back onto her feet. He swung her around.

"I've been miserable since she left me. Can't eat. Can't sleep. Can't concentrate. Hell, I can't even go home. I've been living on an airplane. My only option if I don't want to go crazy is to chase her until she lets me catch her."

Panic made her heart pound, and a surreal floating sensation took over. Crashing into reality was going to hurt. Bad. "If you think that's funny, then you have a sick sense of humor, Faulkner."

"There's nothing funny about me being blind and not seeing what was right in front of my face. There's nothing funny about hurting the woman I'd fallen in love with because I was too scared to face the truth."

Dizziness swamped her. She clung to the door frame. "You fight dirty."

His smile widened and his eyes glinted with mischief. "You haven't seen anything yet. Give me a chance to regain your trust, Lauren. Let me prove I love you."

She identified the weightless sensation as hope and tried without success to snuff it. "How are you going to do that?"

"I'm not sure, but if I keep trying new strategies for the next fifty years or so, I'm sure I'll hit on a winning combination sooner or later."

He cupped her cheek, stealing her breath and making her eyes sting. "I love you, Lauren. I love that you're genuine and honest. You don't pretend to be someone you're not. I love that you appreciate the simple things instead of going for the bling. I love that you have enough pride to insist on earning what you have, and that you're stubborn enough to stick to your guns when you know you're right.

"But most of all, I love that you're generous enough to share your gifts with me."

Her cheeks burned. She swiped at them and found tears. *Pilots don't cry, damn it.*

Gage caught her soggy hand in his. "We haven't known each other long. We'll take it as slow as you want. I want to learn everything there is to know about you. But I already know the important part. That I love you and want to spend the rest of my life with you. Promise me you'll give me that chance."

Emotion welled up in Lauren's throat. She wanted to laugh. She wanted to cry. But more than anything she wanted to smack Gage for putting her through missing him.

She yanked her hand free and slugged him in the upper arm, not hard, but enough to show her frustration. "If you'd figured this out sooner, I wouldn't have had to live through almost a month of hell."

Gage's laugh boomed out, echoing off the metal hangar walls. "I hope our kids are as spunky as you."

"Kids? Getting ahead of yourself, aren't you?" Then the smile she couldn't contain burst free. "How many?"

"A hangar full."

He yanked her into his arms and kissed her hard once and then his mouth opened over hers. Lauren opened to him, opened her mouth, opened her heart, opened her life. He tasted so good, so familiar, so welcome, and she couldn't get enough of him.

Her clipboard clattered onto the concrete floor. She wound her arms around Gage's neck, tangled her fingers in his hair and poured her love into the kiss.

When dizziness threatened to make her faint in his arms, she lifted her head and cupped his cheeks. "I love you, too. And nothing would make me happier than spending the rest of my life with you."

* * * * *